FNNF-able

a novel by

Marshall Evans

Printed in the United States of America
First Printing, 2017

ISBN 978-0-9970127-6-7

Land's Ford Publishing
Spartanburg, SC, USA

Cover photo remixed from Livioandronico2013, Wikipedia Commons
Author photo courtesy of Sam Hillers

To Ish Barbee

il miglior fabbro

You know how this works. It's a novel. I made it up. It would be marvelous if my friends and family could read this book without asking what parts of the story are true.

I may hope for too much.

Lately, I ran into one of my ex-relatives at the grocery store. He enjoyed my first novel, he said, but he kept wondering how much was true. He suggested publishing a red-letter edition, with the true bits printed in red ink.

What a charming idea! As if printing pieces of a story in red could quell whatever yearning is driving these readers. They may seek truth where it simply does not lie.

This is fiction. Once you jump in with your imagination, aren't you just as responsible for whatever comes of it?

By way of disclaimer: the part about Wachovia Bank is all true, at least according to the newspapers.

For there are some eunuchs, which were so born from their mother's womb: and there are some eunuchs, which were made eunuchs of men: and there be eunuchs, which have made themselves eunuchs for the kingdom of heaven's sake.
 - *Jesus*

Cupid himself would blush to see me thus transformed.
 - *The Merchant of Venice*

TRIGGER WARNING

The characters in this book are endowed by their creator with genitalia. They use them as you might imagine.

And language... What really can be said? Dare we dream ourselves intrepid rangers on that frontier?

1

She was so shockingly beautiful. How could he be thinking about that now? How could he still be obsessed?

The cinnamon skin. The tacky hair extensions. The breasts. Oh how they danced in that wife-beater t-shirt! How obscenely exposed!

Her uncaring disdain!

It was driving him mad. Here in this place. With this bastard and his insane plans to mutilate and kill.

Tony Jones had loved her so. Longed for her. She was the stuff of his daydreams. The dreams he never admitted to anyone.

And the song, damn it! The refrain stuck in his mind. *The Theme from Shaft.* Why was that stuck in his mind?

Tony suddenly realized how appropriate the song was. He chuckled.

They glared at him, with a brief look of wonder. Only so brief.

"Cha," the bastard said. "Why don't you pull that little white dick out on the chair for us? Stretch his balls on out there, too."

A smile came to her face.

The bastard now picked up a bread knife from the table behind him. About a foot long. Black plastic handle. Stainless blade. Deep serrations.

The two attendant thugs grabbed Tony's shoulders like he was about to be crucified. Tony's ankles were duct-taped to the chair legs. Duct tape held a rubber ball in his mouth. Tony didn't struggle. He sat, naked and bound and exposed, as she reached for his crotch.

"He's always dreamed of me touching it," she said.

"Not as much as I've dreamed of this," the bastard said. He ran his index finger along the serrations of the bread knife. He accidentally cut himself and winced.

She grabbed Tony's penis and cupped her fingers under his gonads. She looked Tony in the eye and smiled.

"Drag his ass out to the edge of that chair," the bastard said. "Get me a little sawing room."

She yanked. The two thugs drove Tony's upper arms downward. Tony moaned into the rubber ball.

The cell phone on the table rang. The ring tone was *The Theme from Shaft*. The bastard turned.

"What the fuck does that bitch want now?" Deuteronomy said. He continued to hold the knife aloft as he poked the screen on his iPhone 3g.

2

Two-hundred eighty-two days earlier:

Tony was staring out his office window, daydreaming of Chaqueena as usual. Oh, if anyone ever knew what his daydreams were.

He leaned back in his leather chair, ankles crossed on the credenza, and looked over the tall buildings in his corner of downtown Charlotte, across the slums beyond them, and onward to the coves of Lake Norman gleaming in the distant haze.

Where did the longing come from? Whenever he had a spare moment he imagined making love to her on his huge desk. Right there in the office. As if she would ever come in that office. As if he would ever dare.

She's a Brick House. The song by the Commodores was the theme music of this daydream. It always played in his imagined encounters with Chaqueena.

Tony waggled his head a little and hummed the opening line to himself.

The door opened. He tried not to look embarrassed.

Swati stuck her head in the office. She looked so serious. Was she always so serious? Tony wondered. He was aware of how he had been grinning.

3

"Your brother..." Swati said. She opened her eyes wide. She held the door closed against her shoulders.

"What about my brother?" Tony asked, irritated.

"What the fuck do you mean, what about your brother?" Tony heard a voice booming from the corridor just beyond the door.

"Oh shit!" Tony mouthed silently to Swati. He waved his hands in front of his face. She held the door mostly closed and turned outward.

"Don't you even start that crap with me," his brother's voice roared. "What, you got some big deal going on in there? Got millions of dollars to make? Can't be seen with your little brother?"

"Swati, just let him in," Tony said.

The door opened to reveal a middle-aged man, six-foot-four, two-hundred-forty-pounds, sandy-haired.

"I have real business meetings in here," Tony said. "Actual important shit."

"You're in here daydreaming about porn flicks," Bass said.

Swati hurried away.

"Seriously, dude," Tony said.

"Seriously dude my ass."

Bass plopped into a guest chair like it was the couch in their childhood home.

"Appointment?..." Tony said. "Call in advance?..."

"Kiss my balls."

The pitch of Tony's voice went up. "Bass..."

"Oh, I'm just fucking with you." That damned smile. "Listen."

"You need money."

There was a silence here. The smile vanished. Tony could see his brother fighting to control anger.

"For Christ's sake, Tony," Bass said.

"Am I wrong?"

"There's no need to just blurt it out like that."

Tony allowed himself to revel in his brother's anguish a bit. Tony adopted his ingratiating, condescending tone. "You can just ask. I really don't mind."

Bass looked like he was being offered a turd on a platter.

"I've got more of it than I could ever need," Tony said. "I mean really, it means nothing to me at this point."

"Jesus," Bass said.

"I just want to help," Tony said. "I don't expect to be paid back. We know that by now, don't we? Seriously, I don't want to talk loan. It's a gift. You may be able to do the same for me some day."

"I'm not asking for a handout here," Bass said.

Tony held his hand up to cut his brother short. "I don't care, Bass. I don't give a shit. I love you. You're my brother. I want to help." Tony opened his desk drawer and pulled out a checkbook.

"Hold on," Bass said.

"I am being perfectly honest with you," Tony lied to his brother.

"Tony," Bass said, "would you listen to what I have to say?"

Tony looked at his watch. "I've got ten minutes," he said, sitting back in his chair. "Then I really have to go. Got to catch a plane to Chicago."

"Catch a plane? I thought you owned the plane."

"I've got to make it to the goddamned meeting in Chicago on time. O.k. How much do you need?"

"I've got a way to end this," Bass said. "I can put a stop to all this."

"You know," Tony said, smiling his ingratiating smile, "maybe business just isn't your thing, Bass. What if that's the case? I mean who gives a shit? At the end of the day, at the end of our lives, who the hell is really going to care about that? Do we really have to go on investing in these things? There's enough here you could just come to me whenever you need to, and frankly, it's a lot cheaper to help you out directly than to invest in a business that's not going to pan out."

"I'm not talking about an investment," Bass said. "I'm talking about marrying for money."

Tony laughed before he could stop himself. "Portia Stephens?" he said. "That's your plan?"

"You have no idea," Bass said.

Tony just shook his head.

"She's a beautiful girl," Bass said. "She's exquisite. And she's so damned nice."

Tony listened. He didn't disagree.

"And you know perfectly well she could fall for me," Bass said.

Any girl could fall for Bass, Tony thought. The trouble was they just kept on falling. Sooner or later they hit the ground, woke up, shook themselves off, and walked away.

What was it about Bass? He was a brilliant man. Nobody would deny that. He had the graduate degrees to prove it. Not degrees leading in a progression toward a terminal degree, mind you, but more Master's degrees from the nation's finest schools than anyone ought to have. And he was a good-looking bastard, damn it. Even now, near forty, with the extra weight on him and the receding hairline, he was damn good-looking.

Why couldn't he get it together? He got the great jobs. He got the great ideas. He charmed people. But it never worked out. He was always in debt. He was always needing money.

Like Thomas Jefferson, Tony Jones reflected. But Jefferson did something with his damn life. Thomas Jefferson wrote the Declaration of Independence and was President of the republic and fathered all those black children. Tony was beginning to drift off now thinking about Jefferson mounting his lovely mulatto slave, perhaps on his Presidential desk, when Bass slapped the desk in front of him.

"Goddamnit, Captain A.D.D.! Listen to me."

"Hey, I've got to catch a plane," Tony said, standing up.

"All right, here's the pitch," Bass said, chopping his open hand at his brother. "Tune in for one minute."

"I'm all ears." Tony remained standing.

"Portia is a dream babe. Everybody knows it," Bass said.

"Oh, come on," Tony said. "I hear she's effanineffable."

Bass was bewildered. "She's what?"

"Effanineffable," Tony said.

His brother threw his hands up in frustration. "What the hell does that mean?"

"Fucking in-fuckable," Tony said.

"In-fuckable? What are you talking about?" Bass said.

"Hell if I know. It's just what I've heard over the years. Effanineffable."

Bass thought slowly and ponderously. "Well, maybe that explains it," he said.

Tony was paying attention now.

"Hey, you know," Tony said, "I just hear there's some major reason nobody stays with her. No idea what it is. You just hear..."

"You don't have a clue," Bass said. "There's a lot more to this than you imagined."

"Like what?"

"Portia's father was a manipulating bastard," Bass continued, "but he was rich as hell, and he loved Portia the way you love me."

Tony didn't bother to remonstrate.

"So here's the deal," Bass said. "Portia invited me out to her place on Figure Eight this weekend. I go. She's a great girl. I mean I thought it might be some good friend-fucking coming up at the beach, but now that you mention that... Well , it turns out she's got something much more important in mind. Turns out it's a business proposition."

At the word "business," Bass was starting to lose Tony.

"Nothing like you're thinking," Bass continued, standing up to block Tony's movement toward the door. "You're not going to believe this. Portia is heiress to a one-point-four-billion-dollar estate, and she can't get her hands on it without my help."

Tony stopped as if Bass had grabbed him by the crotch.

"I'm listening," Tony said.

"Stephens' will," Bass said, "it put all the money in a trust, and Portia got nothing- nothing except the use of the beach house on Figure Eight and a condo in Raleigh. Plus a couple of weeks a year at the mansion up in Edgartown. And you know her, that's enough for her. She's got her teaching job. She's not a vain person at all. But Stephens laid out some bait for her. He put in a mechanism by which she could get her hands on the whole thing, but only if..."

And Bass just stopped. He let the silence hang. The silence had the desired effect on his brother.

"What? Goddamnit! Only if what?"

"He designed what he thought would be the perfect marriage scheme for her. Poor bastard. Gonna run her life from the grave. You wouldn't think Portia would let it get to her. I don't think the money alone would get to her. But she loved him, Tony, and she misses him like there's a great big hole in her heart. This scheme of his is a way she can connect, I think."

Tony just listened now. This is what Bass could do to him. It's what Bass could do to anyone. Why did it never work out? It was always based on the truth, on the real desires and concerns of the human heart, but it never seemed to work out like you'd think it should.

"She can get the whole fortune," Bass continued, "but only if she marries. The marriage has to meet certain conditions and continue to meet them for the rest of her life. Otherwise, she has to forfeit the full fortune AND- and she loses the house and the condo."

"How the hell could he set that up?" Tony asked. "Once she gets her hands on the money, how can he ever get it back from her?"

"Nested trusts. One trust is nested inside the other. One pays the other. She can become the trustee of the parent trust if, but only if she meets the conditions stipulated in the will."

Tony wasn't sure he followed this. He was fairly certain Bass didn't really understand what he was talking about, but the story was just far enough beyond Bass's capabilities to sound feasible. Tony listened.

"She must marry a man with at least ten-million dollars in liquid assets at the time of their marriage. He also has to own a house on Figure Eight Island free and clear- so that's at least an-other two million. And he has to sign a prenup- the prenup's al-ready drawn up by Stephens. It stipulates the man will lose ev-erything he has- everything- in the case of a divorce, whether the divorce is sought by either party. He loses everything he has going into the marriage, plus everything Portia brings in- it all has to be donated to the Raleigh YMCA if they ever divorce."

"The fucking YMCA?" Tony said.

"The YMCA," Bass said.

"That's insane," Tony shouted.

"It may be," Bass said, "but it's true. She had me briefed by the estate's lawyers in Durham."

9

"What? Why didn't you let me know this?" Tony shouted. "You didn't sign anything, did you?"

"No," Bass said. "I'm not a dumb ass. It was all very businesslike. Very discreet. Very gentlemanly. I'm not the first to have been briefed, apparently."

"Jesus," Tony said. "It's fucking nuts." He thought for a moment. "Listen, so she does this as a marriage of convenience. I mean, for that much money, who gives a damn?"

"Oh, you won't believe it," Bass continued. "Stephens had it all worked out. Pinkerton Security Services has to certify every six months- for the life of the marriage- that the couple is living together, sleeping regularly in the same bedroom, or everything is taken away."

Tony laughed.

"And," Bass continued, "Pinkerton has to certify that neither party has committed adultery. They have to do this every six months for the rest of their married lives. Pinkerton has to stalk them like private detectives. Well, they are private detectives. If they find adultery, the gig is up."

"Jesus!" Tony was pacing behind his desk.

"And the couple has to have children. They have to have three children on their own. Or they have to adopt. Within ten years of the marriage."

"This is the wildest thing I've ever heard," Tony said.

"Think about it just a little," Bass said. He paused. "Think how Portia Stephens would have to feel about someone in order to marry them."

Tony thought.

"You've got to catch a plane," Bass said. "We'll talk later." He stood up.

Tony was speechless.

"Portia has asked me to marry her," Bass said. "Under those conditions."

Tony just stared at him.

"And I need the money and the beach house," Bass said.

3

When Tony got on the plane, he realized he had no idea where he'd just parked his Maserati.

He was consumed by the Portia Stephens deal.

Was it because this presented an opportunity to get Bass off his back?

Was it because Tony couldn't stand to see his brother succeed?

Was it because Tony wanted to get his own hands on the Stephens family fortune?

Tony liked to have other people's motives clear in his mind before he acted. Bass's and Portia's motives were clear to him. They wouldn't care about the money. They cared about the marriage. They wanted the marriage and the kids and the success and the love of the dead father. Tony could see through people. He did it every day. He wasn't having any trouble analyzing Bass's and Portia's motives.

It was his own motives that were mystifying. He couldn't clarify his own motives. Tony was wrestling with that part of it.

Tony was flying to Chicago to arrange mezzanine financing for an office tower. This new project would block the view from his current office. Tony knew it would outshine any other downtown skyscraper in Charlotte. It would tower over the shady neighborhoods to the north, beaming forth the hope and power of capitalist expansion- a beacon of white success glaring over the dark people plotting their petty crimes below.

Tony thought of Chaqueena hanging from Deuteronomy's arm at the very tony, very private Apex Club downtown. A drug-dealing pimp at the Apex Club bar. Jeez, Tony thought, what Tony Jones wouldn't do for money.

Money was the thing driving him crazy about the Portia Stephens deal. If he could get the cash, he'd front Bass the twelve million immediately. No, hell, twelve million wouldn't do it. A decent house at Figure Eight would probably cost four or five. Something Portia could be seen in. And Bass might blow through some amount of cash before the deal could be consummated. It probably needed fifteen or sixteen.

But there was no way. Tony couldn't come close. He had the net worth, of course. What was his latest claim- the latest bullshit on the financial statement? North of a hundred million, for sure. But he'd be hard pressed to come up with two million in cash. It was all tied up in deals.

He could borrow. He only needed to come up with a viable story. He couldn't tell a banker what he was really going to use the money for. An inquiry anywhere along those lines would immediately get back to the Stephens managers and squirrel the deal. He had to come up with some cover story. It had to be good enough to isolate his borrowing completely from Bass's subsequent home purchase and matrimonial balance sheet. Nobody should be able to guess the connection.

These thoughts whirled in Tony's mind for one hour as his plane flew to Chicago. When the pilot told him they would soon be landing at Midway, Tony checked his watch. He wanted to beat Chicago traffic. He hated sitting in limousines.

4

Deuteronomy let go of his Aunt Irma's hand as she raised it in prayer. The choir was hitting the high notes of "Amazing Grace," and Irma was filled with the spirit. Deuteronomy remained seated as his aunt rose to all five feet of her height and swayed with the music, waving her hands above her head.

He sat with her every Sunday. It was his thing. When he was in Charlotte, he would no more have missed it than miss a chance to make a dollar.

He missed neither.

Deuteronomy was not, however, thinking of amazing grace at this particular moment. He was thinking of the trip he and Chaqueena had taken to South America two days prior. He was thinking of his Gulfstar Intercontinental, and how that prick Tony Jones only had a Learjet.

He hated Tony Jones.

Jones with his understated mansion in Myers Park. The fucking oak trees out front must be a hundred years old. The fucking white neighbors were damn near as old.

Deuteronomy knew he could dress in a t-shirt and sweats, walk down the sidewalk in that neighborhood, and within three minutes a cop car would pull up alongside him, flashing its blue lights.

Tony Jones hated him, too, Deuteronomy knew. Sure, the two men shared a love of money. Sure, they both could buy whatever they wanted and do whatever they wanted. Sure, they could both do business at a level few other men in Charlotte could. They could stare into each others' eyes and know neither would blink. They could read- or they could tell themselves they could read- each others' minds. And they shared the same consuming level of self-doubt that terrified them and made them hide behind that facade of power.

Jackson knew it, at least, sitting beside his Aunt Irma in the Grace and Faith Tabernacle on the North side of Charlotte that hot, Sunday afternoon.

Fuck that Tony Jones, he thought.

"When we've been there ten thousand years," the choir sang, "bright shining as the sun..."

"Oh Jesus," his aunt cried out.

Deuteronomy stared at her as he always stared at this mystery.

And he asked God to please, please save him.

He meant it. He always did.

5

Portia and Nerissa propped their bare feet on the porch railing at Figure Eight Island. They both had hiked their skirts up to their crotches to get some sun on their thighs. And they were drinking bottled beers.

Portia was in her late thirties. She was strikingly beautiful, the kind of woman who draws unconscious stares when she walks in public. She was tall and blond and voluptuously athletic, but she was also the possessor of a beautiful kind of bearing- the kind of bearing that makes others stop, and yearn, and wonder why they are suddenly feeling that way.

Nerissa was a brunette of about the same age and build. She was a pretty woman, but she did not have that bearing, and people did not stop to stare at her.

Portia's house towered over the sand dunes, the empty beach beyond them, and the curling waves of the Atlantic beyond that. An offshore wind was fighting an eight-foot swell rolling from a storm beyond the Gulf Stream.

"Combing the white hair of the waves blown back," Portia said, "When the wind blows the water white and black."

"We have lingered in the hidden chambers of the sea," Nerissa responded.

"With sea-nymphs, wreathed by red and brown."

"Till human voices wake us, and we drown."

They were silent a bit, but the sea wasn't.

"Effanineffable," Portia said.

"What?" Nerissa said.

"It's T. S. Eliot, too. From 'The Naming of Cats,'" said Portia.

"I do remember that one. The cats have some secret name that only they know. It's like the ultimate mystery of the universe."

"Effanineffable," Portia said.

"It's so fucking ineffable," Nerissa said.

And they were silent as the wind blew white wisps backwards from the wave tops.

"You may have too much poetry," Nerissa said.

"Is that possible?" Portia asked.

"Sure. you can have too much of that."

"I may have too much money," Portia said.

"That you may well have, also."

Another silence. This one longer. When the swells curled and broke, a muffled thump sounded far away.

"Bass Jones," Portia said. "Of all the ones."

"There have been many," Nerissa said. "Jesus, there have been many."

"I was embarrassed to tell him," Portia said. "Bass, that is. Not embarrassed to tell him about the will, so much. Embarrassed to tell him about the others. I felt cheap. I felt like a fallen woman."

Both women laughed.

They stared out at the sea. A prosperous-looking couple walked on the beach with a Golden Retriever. The beach was nearly empty this morning. A lone man strolled four hundred yards or so to the south and a group of preppy, college-aged kids jumped and ran a hundred yards or so to the north.

The couple looked up to Portia and Nerissa and waved as they passed.

"Do I know them?" Portia asked.

"I don't think so," Nerissa said.

"Oh, I think I met them at the Yacht Club," Portia said. "This week. They're from Richmond. He's an investment banker. Sophie Turner's kid works for him."

"She's pregnant, you know."

"Sophie?" Portia asked, giggling.

"No, the daughter. She's married."

"She's a child."

"She's of appropriate child-bearing age, darling."

"Unlike some of us."

And there was a long silence here. They drank their beers.

"I'm terrified," Portia said.

"I know you are."

6

The fairway sloped steeply uphill and doglegged left. Bass teed up and took a graceful swing.

It was a spectacular golf shot- three hundred yards, hooking around the dogleg. The ball flew in an elegant, effortless curve and rolled to a stop in the middle of the fairway.

"Fuck you," his best friend Gray said.

Gray bent to tee up his shot.

"Not a bad shot, really," Bass said.

"Would you please just lick my balls?"

Gray's tee shot was far short of Bass's, wide on the edge of the rough to the right.

Their friend Lorenzo was waiting for them in one of the carts.

"So how long you been doing this black chick?" Gray asked Lorenzo as he climbed behind the wheel.

"Dude," Lorenzo said, "I'm serious about this. This is a serious thing."

"The kind you don't take home to mama?" Gray said.

"I have, as a matter of fact, taken her home to mama. Several times," Lorenzo replied.

"She is hot," Gray said.

"A creature of infinite beauty. Far your intellectual and professional superior, I might add."

"Do you have to add that?" Gray said. They took off down the cart path.

Their cart rolled to a stop beside Lorenzo's pathetically placed tee shot. He faced at least two more strokes to get to the green- they both knew. Bass stopped his cart behind them.

"Bass," Lorenzo said, "will you make him stop talking about my girlfriend? I'm trying to play golf."

"Is her father really Deuteronomy Jackson?" Bass said.

"Yes."

"Jesus. Beautiful and rich," Bass said.

"She hates Deuteronomy," Lorenzo said. "Has nothing to do with him."

Bass knew Lorenzo's head was a mess, now. He sat quietly and watched Lorenzo shank his shot into the woods.

"Jesus," Lorenzo said.

"Give him a beer," Bass said.

Bass sped away in his cart.

"He fucks with your head," Lorenzo said.

"You want to fuck with his head?" Gray said.

"How?"

"Show him this." Gray went to his golf bag and fished a piece of paper from a pocket.

Gray took the paper to Lorenzo and unfolded a color photograph torn from a pornographic magazine.

"What the hell is that?" Lorenzo said.

"I mean... What about that?" Gray said.

"Is that...?"

"A chick with a dick," Gray said.

"Is that even possible? That can't be real."

"Ambiguous genitalia."

"What?"

"Sure. There's people born that way," Gray said. "Show Bass that. He won't hit a decent shot for the rest of the front nine."

After Lorenzo shared the photo with Bass, Bass three-putted the next green. He was eight over par when they made the turn to the back nine.

7

(Note to Reader: You may find some of the dialogue in this chapter opaque, banal, impenetrable. But this is how these characters talk. This is really how finance at this level is done. In fact, for the rest of this book, you should attribute boring, vulgar, racist, or inappropriate passages to your writer's extensive experience in the real world. The easy-to-believe parts are just fiction.)

Tony Jones sat in the lobby of the Palmer House Hilton with the GE Capital guy. Tony knew how to work this wage slave. The guy would never have the kind of money Tony had. Tony knew it and the wage slave knew it. It was important for Tony to send little reassuring signals to the GE wage slave that this was the case. Flying up here in his Learjet was one signal. There was just the slightest reference to the flight at the beginning of the conversation. Just enough to be noticed.

Now Tony was drinking chamomile tea, which he had ordered with grated cinnamon. He knew this was a silly choice. He really didn't even like it that much. But it had to be done. It was like the toy soldier collection he kept on the walls of his office. It had to be there because nobody else would have one of those collections, and the little soldiers, painted in uniforms of different countries and different periods and different wars, carrying different types of manual arms, were just the sort of thing that would throw visitors off. Were they expensive? Were they rare? Had the visitor ever heard of people collecting such things? If the visitor asked- and they almost never did- Tony was ready with a story and the name of the Hollywood celebrity who first shared with Tony his passion for collecting soldiers. But it was mostly bullshit. Tony just liked toy soldiers, and he knew having a collection of them in his office threw everyone else slightly off guard.

Now, without having to think about this posing too much, Tony drank the bullshit chamomile tea in the lobby of the Palmer House. He treated the GE Capital guy with cool, professional disdain, cloaked in a wealthy graciousness. He answered the younger, female analyst's questions with indulgence. He didn't blink when she questioned the slightly-too-high developer's fee in his proforma, which Tony knew perfectly well would be removed in a haircut at the closing table, but which the young analyst was thinking would be her little coup, which she would proudly present to her boss later, in their private meeting. Tony knew this stuff like his brother knew how to hook a tee shot around a left dogleg. It really didn't take any mental effort at this point, and it damn near bored him.

Except... Except he was really thinking about the Portia Stephens/ Bass Jones deal, and the seed money he was going to need to set up that merger. He was wondering how he might, just might, float the least bit of an exploratory foray into that venture without squirreling this meeting.

So later in the conversation, after the stupid tea had been drunk, and after the hot, young Wharton-grad analyst had convinced herself (mistakenly) that she had impressed the older men with her questions, and when Tony had that feeling that this one was just about in the bag, Tony let himself break loose just the least bit.

"Listen," he said. "Completely different subject. Family friends- wealthy family- wanting to create some liquidity as a cushion. Heavily invested in commercial, downtown office and residential space- Charlotte, Atlanta, Miami. They see the cycle is coming to a close. Looking to borrow fifteen-to-twenty million. Good collateral. Great cash flow. Where's the best place for them to go with that these days?"

"Well," the GE guy said, shrugging. "Last week I would have said we were the people to talk to. But we're starting to see some reluctance now. Don't know. Might be the beginning of a slow-down. If your deal weren't so far into the pipeline, I might even be giving you a little guidance, right now, frankly. I'm thinking if they want that much liquidity in this climate, they're going to find a sale to be more expeditious than borrowing."

"Wow," Tony said. "Well, what can I say? We've all been here before. REIT's still shopping? They still able to place debt, you think?"

"I don't have a good read," the GE guy said. "You know, this could contract fairly hard, you know, with the run-up we've had lately. I think your people should be looking for a REIT with a fresh load of cheap equity. I think there are still some of those around."

"Wow. You're saying they'd be looking to sell at straight eq-uity pricing?" Tony said.

"I might be saying that."

Tony whistled. "Thanks," Tony said. "That helps me know what to tell them."

The GE Capital guy shrugged.

And so, when Tony Jones walked out the front door of the Palmer House into an October afternoon in 2007, he was wondering where in the hell he was going to get his hands on fifteen-million dollars. The bland conversation of the GE Capital guy, so maddeningly dull to the uninitiated, had told him everything. There was no credit. The credit markets were shutting down. Fast.

This was not good. Tony was glad he had three major exit sales inked and well on the way to closing. He would get out be-fore the collapse. He always did.

But the nearest deal closing was at least three months out. Where the heck was he going to get fifteen million right now?

Maybe thirteen, he thought, as he waved to his limo driver. Portia could accept a fucking three-million-dollar beach house.

She could just tear it down and rebuild when she got her in-heritance.

8

In the limousine returning to Midway, Tony was bothered by his whirlwind thinking. He knew he was not being mindful. He knew he was trying to steer this thing with Portia, rather than just letting it happen. He tried to meditate, in the back seat of the limousine, as it was stuck in traffic beside Lincoln Park.

He even bounced his right leg a bit. He had watched a Tibetan monk in saffron robes do this in an airport once. He liked this.

Tony had little formal training in meditation. But he had read a great deal about it. He had practiced it extensively. At last he was able to bring himself into some state of mindfulness and let go of Bass and his marriage deal.

This mindfulness, was, however, as fleeting as ever. He began thinking about Chaqueena. Before he knew it, he felt himself getting an erection.

He chuckled.

Chaqueena. Deuteronomy's bitch. Tony had met Deuteronomy Jackson on the board of the Focus Charlotte Foundation. Jones himself had led the effort to diversify board membership. Jones had stood up in a committee meeting and said, with all due respect, that inviting a couple of black neurosurgeons or attorneys to the board wasn't really diversifying it in this day and age. They needed people who were part of the non-integrated black neighborhoods that made up large sections of urban Charlotte.

He knew this would irritate his fellow board members. Oh, for God's sake, they would think, although they wouldn't dare say it: not another loudmouth Democrat ward heeler, or some black clergyman. They all cringed secretly, while they smiled their correct smiles.

Tony's proposal was designed to blow their smugness apart. He proposed inviting Deuteronomy Jackson onto the board.

The proposal was greeted with a stony silence.

Finally, one member, the general manager of one of the pro sports franchises, spoke out. "Deuteronomy Jackson is a convicted felon," he said.

"And so," Tony said, "are most of the black men who live in his neighborhood." Tony didn't know if this was accurate, but no one challenged him.

Instead, this was met with an uncomfortable shifting of white asses in expensive conference room chairs.

"I mean," the general manager of the sports team said, "think of the message you are sending."

"Think of the message the Panthers send every Sunday," Tony said, "when they fill the football field with young, black men from neighborhoods like that and have them play their hearts out for rich, white Jerry Richardson sitting up in the owner's box. Sure, Jerry makes a few of them kind of rich themselves, but he leaves most of them broke and poor in a couple of years. It's the reality we all live with. We may not be comfortable thinking about it, but we don't mind living with it. And what I'm saying is if we're going to really talk about the future of Charlotte, we need to get some people on this board who can speak out of that reality.

"We all know where Deuteronomy Jackson started out," Tony said. "But has he really ended up in any different place than Mr. Richardson, or me, or Hugh McColl?"

Everybody shifted their asses nervously again. This was because Tony had the audacity to mention himself in the same sentence as those two ridiculously rich, old men. As if... Although in Tony's mind, it wasn't a stretch at all.

"Jackson owns as much real estate in this town as I've developed myself," Tony said. "He's a huge force already in the real estate game here. Not in downtown. Not out to the east or the south. But right in those parts of town where this city has to grow. We can't spread out any more. We've got to use those parts of town that are already here.

"I mean look at what's happening down on South End," Tony continued.

"That's gentrification," someone said.

"You're thinking like it's still the twentieth century," Tony said. "Move in the white kids, shove out the blacks. Is that what you want? You want to just keep pushing these pesky black folk out and move in white college grads? And then the blacks move where? South Carolina?"

The other people on the committee looked at Tony with genuine fear. But that's exactly what he wanted. Only a very rich guy could say things like this and get away with it. It was his secret signal to all of them that yes, he was as rich as they suspected he was. He could say things that were true but that no one else dared to say.

So his buddy Tom Rodham spoke up. Tom had made a fortune in online banking and was now a venture capitalist. He also could say things the others couldn't.

"Hey," Rodham said, "Tony's got a point here. The future of this city has got to include the whole city. That includes the people that live in these neighborhoods, and you know, Tony may be right. Deuteronomy Jackson might be the guy who could get us going in directions we wouldn't dream up ourselves. If you want change, you've got to get outsiders into your organization."

So Deuteronomy Jackson was invited to sit on the board. Tony asked Deuteronomy to dinner at the Apex Club to congratulate him and brief him on what was expected. Deuteronomy showed up in an Armani suit with an open-neck, silk shirt.

Hanging on his arm was Chaqueena.

Chaqueena was wearing a form-fitting evening gown, strapless, flowing to the floor at the toes of her six-inch, platform shoes. Her breasts overflowed at the top, jiggling as she walked. Her nails were an inch long- painted chartreuse. She wore gold hoop earrings at least four inches in diameter. She surely had never set foot in a place like this.

And yet she looked as if she might feel it was beneath her.

Tony had never seen such audacity- such sexual energy. Such haughty disdain. Deuteronomy, who was anything but a small man, looked small beside her.

Tony greeted Deuteronomy with a handshake and a smile. Deuteronomy introduced Chaqueena. Tony reached out his hand.

Chaqueena glared at it as if she might spank it.

Then she took it and squeezed it. "Hi Tony," she said. "I like your club. They let girls like me in here?"

Tony Jones was never the same after that.

Why? He often wondered. He couldn't answer that. It was something deeper and stronger than he could put into words. It came from a place that was wholly familiar and wholly untouchable. It moved him as he had never been moved before.

9

Bass and Portia lay in each other's arms. They had kicked the bedclothes to the floor. The sliding glass door lay open, the surf sounded outside, and the afternoon sea breeze lifted the curtains.

"Are we mad?" Portia said.

"Things like this happen all the time," Bass said. "We're both old enough to know that. Nothing ever turns out like you would imagine it."

Portia snuggled her chin into the crook of his neck.

"There has to be some basis for this hope," Bass said. "I mean, why do we all have this hope bubbling up in us all the time? Why do young people get married? Why do old people get married? Why do people fall in love? Why do people start businesses? Why do people build beach houses where the hurricane just knocked one down?"

"Oh, you fat thing, I love you," Portia said, grabbing Bass by his belly and shaking it.

"Who's fat?" Bass said. "I'm a gifted athlete in the prime of life."

Portia hid her eyes in the pillow beside his shoulder. She began to cry silently. Bass suspected at first she might be crying, and then he felt her start to shake, and he reached and felt the tears on her cheeks. Then she really started sobbing.

Bass stroked her hair.

"What's the matter, babe?" he said.

There was a silence.

"You know you can talk to me about it."

"You're not the first," Portia said.

Bass laughed. "Well I hate to break it to you, but you're not the first either."

"You're not the first to try to marry me."

Bass thought about this. "You told me I wasn't the first to be briefed by the attorneys," he said.

"They weren't just briefed. We were engaged. We were going through with it. There were more than one. I didn't want to tell you. It's too embarrassing. You have no idea how embarrassing it is." And Portia began to cry again.

Bass stroked her hair.

"It's nothing to be ashamed of," he said.

"You have no idea," Portia said. She clutched tightly at Bass.

"You know," Bass said, "I see where you're coming from of course, but..."

"Yeh, but..."

10

Jessica White stormed out the revolving doors of the bank tower. She walked across the entry plaza to her father's limousine, standing illegally at the curb.

Deuteronomy was sitting in the back seat. He rolled the tinted window down as she approached.

"What the hell do you want?" she said.

"Just to see my baby girl," Deuteronomy said.

"Fuck you."

Deuteronomy flashed anger. But he restrained himself. "Not many niggers would said that to my face," her father said.

"Don't you use that word with me."

"You have it any way you want it," Deuteronomy said. "Get in the car."

When Jessica was seated beside her father, the driver raised the partition glass to give them privacy. The car rolled away toward the North. Jessica sat angrily on the far side of the bench seat.

"You can hate on me all you want," Deuteronomy said. "But the fact is, I'm the most powerful black man in this town, and you're my daughter."

"You're a thug," she said. "And I'm an investment banker. You're my father just because you fucked my mother, not because you raised me."

"I was in prison most of that time," Deuteronomy said, uncharacteristically beginning to lose his cool. "And by the goddamn way, what the hell is the difference between an investment banker and a thug?"

"Aarrrgh!" Jessica shouted. She shook her fists in front of her.

"Listen," Deuteronomy said, trying to calm the conversation, "I need your help."

"I will not be involved in any criminal activity," Jessica said.

"I have no intention of involving you in anything that could put your career or your reputation at risk, darling."

Jessica laughed.

"I've been approached by Tony Jones," Deuteronomy said. "He's trying to raise some cash, and he's finding the banks are starting to squeeze his balls."

"He's lucky if they're just squeezing," Jessica said. "They starting to cut lots of developers' balls off."

"He don't look like a desperate man," her father said, "and I know a desperate man when I see one. He say he wants to build up some 'liquidity.'" He snickered.

"What's so funny about that word?" Jessica asked.

"Liquidity," he said. "Motherfucker rich as he is, so goddamn broke he got to come to a drug dealer to get money."

"A former drug dealer, you mean?" asked Jessica.

A beat.

"Listen," Jessica said. "His story sounds right in line with what's going on. Everybody's getting shut off. My question would be what he wants the money for."

"He says it's for family shit."

33

"How much money does he want?"

"Twelve million dollars."

"Holy crap," Jessica said. "He wants twelve million dollars for some 'family stuff? And you've got that much money?"

"The money ain't my problem," Deuteronomy said. "I'm trying to figure out how to structure this so it's a legitimate-looking deal. Like I'm somebody, some legitimate motherfucker like he is."

"Twelve-million dollars? Cash?"

"What the hell are you talking about?" Deuteronomy said. "I thought you were some big goddamn investment banker. Working on billion-dollar deals."

"Yeh, but, but I mean... That's..." Jessica shook her head. "You've got twelve-million dollars lying around you can lend to some white fucker you don't even know?"

"I know him. We're on the goddamn Focus Charlotte Foundation board together. As a matter of fact, he personally invited me to be on the board. Maybe if you paid some attention to your old man, you would know that. You ever read a newspaper?"

Jessica stared at her father. The limousine sped through the ghettos of Charlotte.

11

Tony Jones met his brother in his office.

"This is a bit more complicated than we thought it would be," he said. "But it's doable. It's completely doable."

Bass received this in a moment of silence.

"Three things," Tony said. "First, you know I would do anything for you. You're my brother. Anything I have is yours."

Bass said nothing.

"Second, money is tight. Institutional lenders are tightening up. It's not a good time to be borrowing money."

"Tony, you don't have to do this. Think about it for just a moment. This does not have to be done. I mean face it, Portia and I could live together. We could run off and get married, and to hell with it. We can have three kids, or adopt them, I mean who gives a shit? We don't need that money. Nobody needs that much money. It would probably just end up fucking up our lives."

"No," Tony said, wincing, "I'm not saying it can't be done. Listen, Bass, we're talking about something really important here. This is where you've fallen down in the past. You don't really give a shit about money, and it shows."

Bass said nothing.

"And Bass, as much as I love you, you have hurt a lot of people with that attitude over the years. Think how much hurt you have caused."

Bass said nothing. He stared out the window across North Charlotte.

"We can do this. This is not the kind of thing I've ever told you before, but I might as well tell you now. I've got three sales under contract. They close within next three quarters. Everything will be done in the next nine months. It's a lot of money. A lot of cash."

"How much?" Bass said.

Tony hesitated. He really didn't want to tell his brother.

"Tony, Portia is going to want to know. We're not going to let you go out on a limb or endanger everything you've ever built for this. We're just not going to do it. Fifteen million dollars is an absurd amount of money. And how are you ever going to get it in my name without some enormous tax bill?"

"First," Tony said, and he stared his brother ferociously in the eyes, "Portia Stephens doesn't need to know my business. Nobody knows my business. Are you clear about this?"

"Jeez," Bass said.

There was a long silence. Tony looked furious.

"Okay," Bass said.

"Sixty-six million dollars," Tony said. "That's my take. Cash. Clear. Coming from three closings. Any two of them fall through, the third covers the whole deal easily."

"Jesus!" Bass said. "Sixty-six million dollars?"

"The world has changed. Money doesn't work the way it used to," Tony said. "Listen, I know it's absurd. I've worked hard. I've been tough. I've kept going when I wanted to curl up in the fetal position, but who the hell deserves that kind of money? I know it. Everybody knows it. Why shouldn't I help you and Portia out?"

"What about taxes?" Bass said. "What are the taxes on that?"

"I've got loss carry-forwards, investment tax credits on the new deals, depreciation on the old. I won't even pay taxes on it."

"No taxes on sixty-six million dollars in income?" Bass almost shouted.

"Happens more than you'd imagine," Tony said.

"Jesus," Bass said.

"The world has changed," Tony said.

Bass was silent for a moment.

"But where are you going to get the money in the meantime?" Bass asked. "If lenders aren't lending? I'm lost in all this."

"I've got a lender," Tony said. "And I want you to go with me to meet him."

12

Deuteronomy Jackson's office was in an abandoned shopping center in Northeastern Charlotte. There was no sign. The entrance was nondescript. Except for the cars in the parking lot, the place appeared to be derelict. Tony and Bass entered through the only door that wasn't boarded up.

They walked into a stark waiting area with three black, vinyl chairs, their covers torn in places. There was a bullet-proof payment window to one side, with a speaker in the middle of it. Within thirty seconds of their arrival, Chaqueena appeared on the other side of the window. She was wearing a tube dress that was too small. She smiled, reached out with fake fingernails, pressed a switch, and said, "Hi you doin, Tony?"

"Hello," said Tony, with a ridiculous smile. "I didn't know you worked with the man."

"Who you got with you?" Chaqueena asked.

"This is my brother, Bass. Deuteronomy's expecting both of us, I believe."

Chaqueena didn't act as if she had heard what Tony said.

A steel security door buzzed at the far end of the space. She waved them through it.

Inside was the vacant interior of an abandoned supermarket. Empty rows of grocery shelves disappeared into the darkness. A black thug, carrying an Uzi machine gun, greeted them in this area.

"Tony Jones?" the thug said.

"Yes."

"My name Lancelot. I work for Mr. Jackson."

"Lancelot?" Bass asked.

"Yes, that is my name," Lancelot said.

Lancelot told them to follow. He was in no way friendly. His biceps were the size of Bass's thighs.

After a 200-foot walk through the darkness, the thug led Tony and Bass through another security door into Deuteronomy's office.

That's where Bass was amazed to see Jessica.

She was just as shocked.

"Bass?" she said.

Bass laughed. He walked boldly toward Jessica, wrapped his arms around her and kissed her on the cheek. "Darling," he said.

Tony said, "You two know each other?"

"Very well," said Bass. "Jessica, this is my brother, Tony. Tony, this is Lorenzo's girlfriend- can I say that? Jessica White."

Deuteronomy rose from an armchair to shake his visitors' hands.

The office could have been a CEO's office in one of the bank towers, Tony thought. The furnishings were tasteful, outrageously expensive, and understated. The art work appeared to cost millions. But there were no windows.

Where are his toy soldiers? Tony wondered. He was looking for the toy soldiers, or whatever bullshit Deuteronomy would have to throw his visitors off balance. He couldn't find it.

Maybe the daughter was Deuteronomy's toy soldier collection.

Jessica shook Tony's hand, spoke his name, and it was as if he were in a conference room at Goldman Sachs.

The analysts at Goldman always impressed Tony. He thought of them as the ultimate financial professionals. They were in a league of their own, he thought. Did Jessica work at Goldman? Had Deuteronomy hired Goldman for this little deal?

"Jessica is an investment banker," Deuteronomy said. "She don't work for me. I just asked her here to do her daddy a favor."

"This is a rather personal matter," Bass said.

"Bass, we'll be o.k." Tony said, silencing his brother with his hand. "I appreciate the help, Jessica."

"So twelve-million dollars for two-hundred-seventy days," Deuteronomy said.

"Yes," Tony said.

"I was just a bit puzzled about the collateralization," Jessica said.

"The proceeds go directly to Bass Jones as a loan. Family matter," Tony said. "I'm suggesting LIBOR plus four hundred basis points, but we want to hear your thoughts on that. The collateral is my personal guarantee for the full credit. But I need to structure this off my balance sheet."

"Do you have a vehicle in mind?" Jessica asked.

"I do, but I'd like to hear what ideas you have, also," Tony said. "I'm very grateful to your father for considering this. As a personal favor."

"What the fuck?" Deuteronomy said. "Are you two speaking Chinese?"

"I'm sorry," Tony said.

"Daddy," Jessica said, trying to hide her exasperation.

"Now, listen," Deuteronomy said. "Twelve million dollars is a butt load of cash. I ain't got that kind of cash. Ain't nobody got that kind of cash. But the fact is, I can get my hands on it. I got a few brothers got more cash laying around than you two would ever imagine. And they'll let me hold it. And frankly, they ain't going to want no paper trail tracking this shit all over the universe. What they going to want to know is are they going to get their money back."

There was a silence here.

Tony reached into a leather brief he had carried under his arm and pulled out three, bound presentation booklets. He handed them to Jessica.

"I've got three closings under contract within the next two hundred and seventy days. Any one of them will yield me enough cash, after taxes, to repay you in full."

Jessica took the booklets, shuffled them, and read the front covers.

"Tony," Deuteronomy said, "what I asked is, are they going to get their money back?"

"Yes," Tony said, staring Deuteronomy in the eyes. To Tony, this meant one thing. To Deuteronomy, though, this meant something else entirely, and Tony wondered, months afterward, months after he had learned so very, very much more about Deuteronomy Jackson, if this had been the moment when things began to go wrong.

"What the fuck you going to do with this money?" Deuteronomy said, his eyes locked into Tony's gaze, neither man blinking. Tony was enjoying this game. He held the stare even though his instincts told him to stop it, the instincts that saw a rage building in Deuteronomy's eyes. Some sort of distant, dangerous rage that Tony had never really seen before.

Tony smiled. "I'm sorry. I can't tell you," he said. "Believe me, I would if I possibly could. But what I can tell you is this. Ten million dollars will go immediately into T-bills."

Tony saw the rage flaring. He glanced toward Jessica.

"Your daughter will tell you that's as good as putting it in the bank," he said. He smiled at Deuteronomy. "But you may well know that."

Deuteronomy obviously did not know what a T-bill was.

"And two million dollars is going to buy a beach house," Tony continued. "So look at it this way. If every deal I have set up to close in the next nine months fell absolutely flat- and NONE of them is going to do that- then we pull the ten million dollars back out of Bass's bank account, where he hasn't touched it, and I can scratch you a check for two million right now, out of my back pocket."

Deuteronomy looked like a coiled spring. Tony had never really seen this sort of body language in a business meeting. But he told himself he liked it. He told himself he liked Deuteronomy Jackson. He liked his style, and he thought he could introduced this man into some serious, high level deals in the future.

"Hmmm," Deuteronomy said. He looked Bass up and down. Bass was lost in this conversation. He was watching the other three as if they were actors in a Shakespeare play. He was marveling at the complexity of the situation. He was delighting in the motivations of each one. He was smiling.

Deuteronomy looked at Bass with astonishment and disgust.

"Jessica, honey," Deuteronomy said. "Take those to Chaqueena's office. You know where that is? Take them over there and look them over and come back and let me know what you think. Shit, you know my baby here don't normally fuck with anything this small. Do you, honey?"

Jessica rolled her eyes at Bass and left the office by the only door. Jackson pushed a button to allow her to leave.

When the door closed behind her, Deuteronomy said, "She a smart little bitch. She probably the smartest person in this room. Been to Harvard Business School. But she ain't as smart as her old man.

"Now Tony," he continued, "I hear what you saying. You got this covered four ways. You got this layered up with so many ways to win you can't see it coming apart. And that's good. You a smart man. You rich as Croesus. You a pillar of the goddamn community. But the fact of the matter is, you over here in the wrong side of town borrowing money from a goddamn drug dealer. So something's telling me, same as it's telling you, they something ain't right here."

Deuteronomy glared into Tony's eyes.

"Two things," Tony said. "Credit markets are tightening up. They're tightening up as hard as I've seen them tighten. Jessica can tell you that."

There was a silence.

Tony finally broke it.

"And I've just run across the best business opportunity I've ever seen," he said.

"If it's that good, maybe I ought to get me a piece of it," Deuteronomy said.

"It's not possible," Tony said. "If it were, I'd let you in. Believe me."

"Why?" Deuteronomy said.

"I can't explain it. Believe me. I can't tell you. There are a number of reasons, but if I tell you about it, it goes away."

"Why's your brother involved?" Deuteronomy said. "I mean, he's a nice fellow, but he ain't exactly setting the world on fire."

"Listen, Deuteronomy," Tony said. "I know what you want. I know where you want to go. I can help you go there. I *will* help you go there. I can deliver. But I can't tell you what this opportunity is, and I can't cut you in on it. If we need to talk about the interest rate, let's talk about it."

"Well, if we're going to do that, how about some loan processing fees?" Deuteronomy said. "And maybe some credit check fees, some appraisals, some deed stamps, you know?" And he burst out a deep, delighted laugh. He loved what he had said.

"We can talk about whatever you want to talk about," Tony said.

"Shit," Deuteronomy said. "You got me. You know what I want. And you and your friends are holding it, and the last I checked, they weren't sharing it with no brothers. No real brothers, that is. No thug niggers."

This again brought silence. Bass broke the silence this time, "Tony," he said, "I'm frankly not very comfortable with this." He looked at his brother seriously. "I'm not comfortable."

"Bass," Tony said, "maybe you ought to go help your friend Jessica."

"No, no," Deuteronomy said. "Let him stay. I want him to stay."

"Deuteronomy," Tony said, "I don't know if you'll believe this. Maybe you've heard it before, but I mean it. I want to help you get exactly what you want. That's what I'm all about."

Deuteronomy chuckled. "I ain't gonna charge you nothing," he said. "I don't want no fees, and I don't want no interest. You helping me out, and I'm going to help you out."

"We're prepared to pay. We expect to pay."

"I don't want your damn interest. I just want your respect."

There was another silence. Bass interjected.

"Well, you've got mine," Bass said.

Tony looked profoundly irritated. "Listen," he said, "this is going to have to be documented. It's going to have to be lawyered. It's not going to look right without interest."

"I don't need no lawyer," Deuteronomy said. "We'll arrange the security like we do here in the hood. It's simple, but it works."

"You're not talking about loan sharking?" Bass said.

Deuteronomy ignored him.

"Well, how do you do it here in the hood?" Tony said, laughing nervously.

"Here's the way it's going to work," Deuteronomy said. "I ain't going to charge you interest, or fees, or nothing. We ain't going to have no contract. We don't need it. You going to pay me the money back, every dime, right on time. I ain't worried about it."

"Good," Tony said. "Because I..."

"You gonna pay it back, on time, and I'm gonna give it back to my friends," Deuteronomy said. "Because if you don't," he stepped quickly into Tony's very personal space, a clear invasion of Tony's space.

With his left hand, Deuteronomy grabbed Tony by the scrotum. "If you don't," Deuteronomy said, "I'm gonna cut your dick and your balls off. I'm gonna stuff em up your ass, and I'm gonna let you scream while you bleed to death."

Tony Jones didn't blink.

"You ever seen a man die that way?" Deuteronomy said.

Tony was speechless.

Bass sat like stone.

Deuteronomy turned and spoke directly to Bass as he continued to hold Tony. "It's something you don't ever forget."

Deuteronomy let go and patted Tony on the shoulder.

"You don't ever forget it," he said.

13

There was a knock on the office door. Jackson walked to his desk and buzzed the door open.

Jessica entered.

Tony and Bass were still shaken.

"We had a little man talk," Deuteronomy said.

"Men are the only ones who can talk about that?" Jessica said.

No one answered her.

"These are solid deals," Jessica said, handing the briefing booklets back to Tony.

"Well," Deuteronomy said, "it looks like he's good for it. I can transfer the money to Bass within a week. I'm assuming this will be done offshore? I'd like to do it in the Bahamas. And then you can move the money around however you like after that. Go through your corporations and LLC's and whatever you high-finance motherfuckers like to do."

There was a pause here.

"Tony," Bass said. "I don't want you to do this for me."

But Tony Jones smiled the biggest smile Bass had seen in a long time.

"I want to do it," Tony said. "This is not a big deal, but it's the most interesting one I've ever been in."

14

Tony Jones was a meticulous man. He couldn't have gotten to his position without being meticulous, he thought. Things could not be left to chance, and when Bass confided in him that there had been other suitors who tried to marry Portia, Tony made it his business to find out who they were and why the deals had fallen through. He wasn't going to borrow twelve million dollars from a loan shark just to let his brother blow it.

Old man Stephens had passed away in 1998, when Portia, his only daughter, was twenty-six years old. Stephens' wife, Portia's mother, had predeceased him. That gave Portia almost nine years now to try to get a marriage deal done and get her hands on the Stephens fortune.

Nine years worth of Portia's private love life to uncover. That was easy enough. Tony started on the gossip circuit.

Few creatures on earth like to gossip more than successful businessmen. Businessmen deliver gossip with the same tone of gravitas the experienced gossiper in any walk of life uses. This tone helps to make up for the gossiper's lack of real knowledge or evidence. And there is the same glee once the failure of the other human being (whether it is a real failure or not) has been established. Business requires the deal maker feel superior to other human beings. Otherwise, how would he actually deserve the huge amounts of money he intends to grab? Gossip is used constantly throughout the day to belittle all others and establish superiority. The superior deserve to win. The inferior deserve to lose.

A few days' gossiping uncovered five possible candidates, all of whom seemed to have been associated with Portia over the past nine years. These men were: Huger LeBon, Archie Falconbridge, Richard Sexton, Prince Marocain, and Ari Gahn.

Tony knew LeBon. A ridiculous Cajun from Baton Rouge. He pronounced his silly first name, Huger, as "you GEE." Old French pronunciation. LeBon had been fopping around Charlotte for fifteen years. He had money- enough to be a regular at the Myers Park Country Club- and a bit of a Cajun accent to boot. But Tony had no idea how he had made his money, and neither did anyone else. All assumed LeBon had simply inherited it. LeBon looked like the kind of fool who would sooner or later blow through that inheritance. Tony had golfed with him, drunk occasionally with him, and dismissed him as a useless tool. He had no trouble seeing LeBon going after the Stephens fortune, but he had a hard time seeing Portia thinking of the man as anything but a well-dressed stiff good for some casual diversion. LeBon did not seem to be a real candidate.

Falconbridge was an Englishman with an annoying habit of talking through his nose. He had a mustache like a World-War-I pilot. Tony knew Falconbridge from Figure Eight Island, where Falconbridge lived full-time. Falconbridge was a regular participant in a high-stakes poker game Tony liked to join on the weekends. Arch was an idiot playing cards. Tony knew Arch spent a great deal of his time chasing and bedding very young women. Falconbridge, Tony quickly surmised from the stories he heard, had been nothing more than a short-lived mistake by Portia.

Everyone on Figure Eight knew Falconbridge had been caught screwing a coed in the control booth of the drawbridge that leads out to the island.

At 2:00 AM one summer weekend, the security guard had been walking from his shoreside guardhouse to the bridge control booth. He was going to open the draw for a tugboat. The story was- when the guard switched on the light in the control booth, both copulators were naked, the coed on her feet and holding her ankles, with Falconbridge thrusting from behind. A couple of college kids happened to be crossing the bridge in an SUV at exactly the right moment. As the scene was illuminated, the drunken girl whirled to attention, allowing for full recognition and identification. Within twenty-four hours, it was the talk of the island.

Tony was amused to think of Portia Stephens' reaction when she learned. Well, this last part was conjecture on Tony's part. But he had a lot of fun with it. He strongly doubted Falconbridge had ever been sent to talk to the Stephens family attorneys.

Richard Sexton was a lush. Dickie. That was what everyone called him at Chapel Hill. He'd been enough of a drunk back then to stand out among college kids. Dickie had been a Deke and a Ghimgoul, the highest levels of the frat scene, and Tony had had no use for him. Well, Dickie probably would have had no use for Tony for that matter, if he even remembered meeting Tony in college. But now they were in their mid-forties. Dickie had three failed marriages. He was a good-looking bastard, for sure. Portia did seem to have a talent for getting her sexual needs met, Tony surmised, as he dug into the gossip. And the bastards were always discreet.

Dickie Sexton. For God's sake. Tony remembered seeing Dickie when they were college kids. Dickie was dashing around a bonfire after the Beat Duke parade. The Betas were burning whichever floats they could hijack from the passing parade. Dickie was in his boxer shorts, and Tony remembered when another drunken frat boy ripped the shorts down. Tony got a glimpse of Dickie's enormous penis. It was the largest penis Tony had ever seen in real life. The kind of sight that sticks with you.

Well, that explained Sexton, Tony figured. But no one would want to be married to that drunk. Dickie surely had never met the family attorneys.

So it was basically down to Marocain and Gahn. Two rather dark-skinned candidates, Tony noted. He himself could identify with Portia's tastes in that respect.

Marocain spoke with some sort of accent. He was from the Caribbean, originally. Tony couldn't really remember where. Somebody told him, but Tony always mixed up foreign countries. Couldn't keep them straight. The guy wasn't all the way white, but he wasn't black, either. Not by a long shot. Sort of debonair and French-sounding. Always well-dressed. Behaved with impeccable manners.

Gahn came from somewhere in the Middle East. Some kind of Muslim. Or maybe he was from Asia. He was vaguely from someplace over there, as far as Tony knew, and he seemed to be possessed of sufficient wealth to meet the requirements of the Stephens will.

15

"Portia," Nerissa said, "why didn't you marry Prince Marocain or Ari Gahn?"

They were walking on the beach at the south end of Figure Eight Island, far beyond where the houses stopped, where the sand dunes stretched toward the inlet. They were turning back toward Portia's house, a couple of miles distant. Fine, white sand blew in diaphanous sheets along the deserted beach. The sheets of sand stung their bare ankles as they walked. The sea churned in gray breakers.

They walked in silence for a bit.

"Why?" Portia said.

"Aren't you worried about it happening again?" Nerissa said.

Portia picked up her pace. Then she turned suddenly around and walked backwards a few paces, facing her friend.

"Two entirely different things," Portia said. "I mean Prince and Ari. Two entirely different things. Not really related."

She turned and walked forward.

"And neither one was remotely like Bass," she said.

"I know that," Nerissa said.

"No, I mean in ways you wouldn't know."

Nerissa giggled.

"No, damnit," Portia said. "I don't mean that. I mean the way you get to know a man when the chips are down. Neither one really knew what they were signing up for. I mean they knew. They weren't idiots. They had advisors. They knew they could lose everything if the marriage failed, but I don't think it really hit them until it was time to walk down the aisle. We'd been to bed, but I don't think..." She didn't finish that thought.

"Even after they had signed the contracts," she continued, "and sat through the meetings with the attorneys and the accountants, and fought it out with their families, none of the reality seemed to have sunk in until they were within a few days of going to church. And then they both fell apart. Two entirely different ways. But they both just fell apart."

"You mean they had breakdowns?" Nerissa asked.

"That's not what I mean," Portia said. "It's like their true motivation came out, and when I saw that, I just couldn't go through with it."

"You were the one who called off the weddings?"

There was a pause here in the conversation. A strong sea breeze whipped their hair and clothing.

"Yes," said Portia. "I stopped them."

Nerissa said nothing.

"Everybody thinks they bailed out," Portia said. "Oh, who the hell knows what everybody thinks. Who cares?"

More of a pause. Nerissa spoke: "What did you say to them?"

"We were at dinner one night," Portia said. "Down at the yacht club. It was the week of the wedding. And Prince made a toast. It was just the two of us. I remember exactly what he said. 'To the man who will get what many men desire.'"

Nerissa looked sharply at her friend.

"Don't you get it?" Portia said. "'To the man who will get what many men desire.'"

52

"Why would a man want..."

Portia threw her hands in the air in bewilderment.

"And imagine how that made me feel," she said.

"Oh darling," Nerissa said.

There was silence, and they walked on.

"I mean I could see how he might look at it that way," Nerissa said, tentatively.

"What do you mean you could see...?" Portia spat.

Nerissa crinkled her nose.

"Well, it was clear as a fucking bell to me," Portia said. She picked up her walking pace and stepped ahead of Nerissa.

Nerissa laughed.

"What are you laughing at?" Portia said.

"You!" Nerissa said.

"Oh for God's sake."

And they both walked on for a while.

"That's all Prince said to you?" Nerissa said.

"Well, let's just say it went downhill from there. Way down-hill. Fast. Two days later it was clear to me this was not a man I could live with. It was like I didn't even really know him. I didn't know him at all."

"And you called the wedding off with less than forty-eight hours to go?" Nerissa said.

"In the nick of time," Portia said, strolling boldly on toward that point far ahead where the beach and the surf line appeared to reach infinity.

16

"I'm trying to remind myself exactly what business this is of yours," Portia said petulantly as she and Nerissa climbed the wooden stairs onto her back deck. The sun was low, casting an organza glow of sunset onto the breakers before them.

"It's precisely none of my business," Nerissa said, "except who's the one who's going to have to hold you and feed you and pour you drinks after you break the next one off? It sure as hell isn't going to be Bass."

Portia spun at her, "So I'm the bitch who's going to ruin this one, too? I just fuck up every relationship I touch. Your weirdo friend."

She opened a glass door, stepped into the house, and slammed it behind her.

Nerissa took a seat outdoors and watched the surf.

Nerissa estimated it would be ten to fifteen minutes before Portia reappeared. It was more like five.

"I'm sorry," Portia said. She pulled a deck chair up beside Nerissa and plopped in it.

"I know how scared you are, dear," Nerissa said. She leaned over and kissed her friend on the cheek. "It's not like I haven't screwed up my share of them. I know it's different. But we all have some... thing..."

The two friends sat a long time in silence, watching the seagulls glide back and forth over the surf line.

"I suppose I screwed it up with Ari, too," Portia said.

Nerissa said nothing.

"I don't know," Portia continued. "There we were, the week before the wedding, and- once again- he said this thing. I don't know why, but it just went all over me. Why would it get to me so much?"

After a while, Nerissa spoke: "What did he say, exactly?"

"'The man who marries you is getting precisely what he deserves,'" Portia said.

"What the hell did that mean?" Nerissa said.

"I mean..." said Portia. "Like I wouldn't be tearing myself up wondering."

"Were you throwing a bitch at him?"

"No," Portia said. "That's what got to me. We were out on his frigging sailboat. I wasn't doing anything wrong. And then it just comes out of the blue: 'The man who marries you is getting precisely what he deserves.'"

"What did that mean?" Nerissa said.

"I mean, yeh."

"That's all he said?"

"You mean like he'd be getting the money he deserved? Like it takes a billion and a half dollars to make it worthwhile to marry you?"

Tears poured down Portia's cheeks. She didn't make any noise.

"I mean, did you ask him for some clarification?" Nerissa said.

There was a long silence here.

"No," Portia said. "I just let it eat at me."

Portia's tanned shoulders began to quake.

Nerissa stood, hugged Portia closely to her and kissed her on the crown of her head.

"You are a beautiful child of God," Nerissa said. "He made you perfect, just as you are."

Portia, still seated, leaned into her and wailed.

"You've got to believe that, Portia."

Portia just screamed at the universe, while her friend held her tight.

17

Gray searched in Bass's refrigerator for a beer. There were plenty of beers in the fridge. Gray was just searching for one that suited his taste. Finally, near the back, he sighted an expensive IPA and fished it out.

"But how big a boat are you thinking of chartering?" he asked, as he strolled back into the seating area. Bass was watching the commercial break in a Carolina/Duke basketball game. "You're talking about all these people- they aren't going to want to sleep crammed together when they hardly know each other."

"It's a hundred and forty-eight feet long," Bass said. "Six staterooms. They allow up to eighty people on board for cocktail parties."

"Jesus," Gray said. "What the hell does that cost?"

"I just feel I owe it to people," Bass said. "I owe it to Portia. And it will help Tony with his business. Think how much they've both done for me."

"But Deuteronomy Jackson?"

"Apparently he owns some island in the Exumas," Bass said. "His daughter's going to be with Lorenzo. He's the guy Antonio's doing business with."

"What? He has an island for drug shipments?"

"I don't know what he has it for," Bass said. "We're just going over for dinner. The captain says we can anchor right off Jackson's island. We're chartering the boat from Jackson."

"It's Jackson's boat?" Gray said.

"I don't know," Bass said. "They've got all these corporations that own these things. You can't tell who's behind it all. He seems to be able to get us a good deal on the charter."

"You do get around," Gray said. The basketball game was resuming on the big-screen television. A Carolina player was passing the ball inbounds.

"Listen," Bass said. "It's not really me, I know. But Tony wants me to do it. He's paying the charter cost."

"Fuck no! You fucking imbecile! Jesus, what is he thinking?" Gray shouted, gesticulating toward the giant screen.

"I think Jessica is even involved in some business with Tony," Bass said.

"I thought Jessica hated her old man. She barely even admits he's her old man."

"I don't know," Bass said. "Who knows?"

"When you say six staterooms- you're talking about bedrooms?" Gray said. "Fuck you!" he screamed at the television. "Jesus, Roy, take the fucking bastard out!"

"I can't watch this shit any more," Bass said. But neither one of them made any move to stop watching the game.

"It's six queen-sized bedrooms, each with its own bathroom," Bass said.

"Yes!" Gray shouted, jumping to his feet.

"Hell yes!" Bass shouted. Gray did a little dance of glee and sat back down.

"That's what I'm talking about," Gray said.

"They can still pull this one out," Bass said. "It's not over yet. They've got time."

"It'll take a miracle," Gray said.

They must have believed in miracles, because they clung to their hope until the very end of the game.

18

Swati cracked open the office door and stuck her head in.

Tony started a bit. He had been daydreaming about Chaque-ena.

"There is someone to see you," Swati said.

"And who would that be?"

Swati lowered her voice slightly. "There is a man to see you." She arched her eyebrows.

"What kind of man?"

"I think he may work for Deuteronomy Jackson."

The unspeakable had been communicated.

"Send him in," Tony said.

Moments later, Jackson's thug, Lancelot, walked into Tony's office. Lancelot stood stiffly near the door, which Swati closed behind him.

"Yes," Tony said. "I remember you. I'm Tony Jackson." He smiled and walked across the office to shake hands.

"Yeh," Lancelot said, looking away.

"And forgive me," Tony said, "I confess I've forgotten your name."

"I work for Deuteronomy," Lancelot said, stepping back from Tony.

"You had a name like a knight," Tony said, searching.

"Listen," Lancelot said. "I want to know. Is what. I don't know. I mean. I were wondering if you ever need somebody like me. You know."

Tony wasn't sure he knew.

"You know," Lancelot said. "Like somebody who know the street."

"I'm not sure what you mean."

"Like I'm good at protection. And I drive Deuteronomy around. I drive his limousine. And his other cars. Whatever he want me to do."

"You must be a very valuable man to him, then," Tony said, retreating behind his desk. He left Lancelot standing at a distance.

"Yeh," Lancelot said. "He a hard man. I mean he a hard mother..." He stopped himself.

Tony didn't respond.

"What I want to know, is can you use somebody like me? You know. I know how to get things done. Or maybe your brother could use somebody like me."

Up to this point, Tony had been thinking only of how to cut this meeting short. He wanted to avoid even the appearance of poaching one of Jackson's employees. But something about the mention of Bass sparked a thought.

An idea began to form. He needed some time to develop it.

"You're talking about leaving Deuteronomy?" Tony said.

"Listen, you don't just walk away from Deuteronomy Jackson," Lancelot said. "But he all into you- and your brother, too. Like your shit don't stink. He all about it, now, and I'm just thinking, you know, if you could use somebody like me. You know, he ain't gonna want to piss you off or nothing. I mean, you hire a nigger..." Lancelot stopped himself again.

"No, no," Tony said immediately. "I know exactly what you mean. I was just kind of thinking the same thing." He reached down to buzz an intercom. "Swati," he said, "come in please."

She appeared right away.

"Swati," Tony said, "this is..."

Lancelot was no help.

"Mr. Rogers, I believe," Swati said.

"I'm sorry, you had a name like a knight," Tony said.

"Lancelot," Lancelot said.

Tony was afraid for an instant. Then he thought this was starting to look like a very good idea.

19

Deuteronomy was dressed in his Sunday finery. It was far too gaudy to be worn at Myers Park Presbyterian Church. But at the Grace and Faith Tabernacle, these clothes announced Deuteronomy as the richest black man in Charlotte, and the ever-faithful nephew of Sister Irma Jackson Regal.

Deuteronomy strode onto the porch of Irma's very modest frame house and rapped on the door.

His daughter opened it.

Jessica was dressed in a green sweat suit. She was wearing bedroom slippers, and her hair was wrapped in a towel.

She said nothing to her father. He stepped in.

"Laud," Irma said, rolling forth from the darkness of the hallway. "You a handsome devil of a man." Irma was wearing a hat that could have been worn in the first class dining room of the Titanic. Her nephew bought her a new church hat every week.

"You got the devil part right," said Jessica.

"Don't you talk about your daddy that way," Irma snapped.

"Where the hell you dragging in here from?" Jessica's father said.

Jessica just looked at him.

"Don't you look at me that way," he said. "Damn investment banker. You a damn investment banker, living with your aunt, dragging in here all hours of the morning after whoring around with your white dudes."

Jessica shook her head, took up a coffee mug, and seated herself in front of the television. A Sunday morning news show was on. She turned up the volume.

"And you ought to get your black ass up and go to church with your aunt," her father continued.

"Buzz, buzz," Jessica said, drawing her feet up on the sofa under her.

"What the..." Deuteronomy stopped himself short. "What do you mean by that?"

"Are we really going to do this, father dearest?" Jessica said.

Deuteronomy looked murderous.

"Come on, pumpkin pie," Irma said, taking her nephew gently by the elbow.

She led him from the house.

As the door closed behind them, Jessica flipped both her middle fingers towards it.

20

Bass bought a chart book of the Exumas and pored over it. He Googled each little cay and read about it on the Internet. He used his fingertips to measure distances. He called the captain six times to discuss logistics.

Unfortunately, his plans began to unravel as the date of departure neared.

Tony had to beg off from the first three days of the trip. Sudden business demands. He would still fly in to Staniel Cay for the second half of the week. He would still send Bass and his friends down on his Lear jet to Nassau.

Then Portia had to back out.

Bass wasn't quite sure what to make of this. Portia said not to make anything of it at all.

"Seriously, babe," Bass said. "This trip is all about you. It's all about us."

"That's the week before my kids' state testing," she said. "If the school weren't in danger of being shut down, I could justify it. But I can't do that to these people. I mean, tell them I'm going off on a mega-yacht with my fiancé? While their jobs are on the line..."

"Should I try to reschedule?" Bass said.

"No, you should just go with your friends and your brother and have a blast," Portia said. "I promise. I'll make it up to you."

So that left Bass, Gray, and Lorenzo- and their dates. And Lancelot.

Bass had quickly grown to like Lancelot. Lancelot had the most outrageous wardrobe. Every time he drove Bass somewhere in Bass's Land Rover, people would turn and stare. Lancelot didn't give a crap. Bass loved it. Plus Lancelot knew more Tar Heel basketball trivia than Bass did.

And most of all, Lancelot had taken Bass to the shooting range.

Lancelot didn't go to a regular shooting range. Lancelot had his special place, way out in the country beyond Concord, several miles down a two-lane, then down a dirt road that disappeared into the pine woods beside a decrepit house trailer. Lancelot stopped the car beside the trailer and blew the horn. He got out, knocked on the trailer door, waited for it to crack open, and said a few words.

A good quarter-mile down the dirt track was Lancelot's shooting range- a bulldozed scar in the red clay hillside, surrounded by deep woods.

Here Lancelot pulled out a duffel full of the most delicious and illicit weaponry. Bass asked Lancelot where he had gotten all these guns.

Lancelot just laughed. Glocks, Smith and Wessons, revolvers, a Lugar you could hide in the palm of your hand. An Uzi. An AK 47. An M16. Not the legal versions. The fully-automatic versions.

Lancelot let Bass shoot the machine guns into the clay bank. He showed Bass how to load them, how to hold them, how to compensate for the recoil.

"This shit will fuck a nigger up," Lancelot said, with laughter in his eyes. Lancelot held the Uzi at hip level and emptied an entire magazine into the clay bank. Fifty rounds in five seconds. The red clay exploded and sprayed, and the outrageous sound died in the deep woods around them.

"I love it," shouted Bass as the sound echoed on the surrounding hills.

21

What would it take to convince you of the perfidy and in-sanity of the world financial markets in the year 2007? You've seen it explained. You've seen it dramatized. You've seen it documented.

Even more, you lived through the end results of it.

But for some reason, the actions of the real people who caused the crisis don't seem that real to you..

Why is that? Are the financial terms too complex? Are they designed purposefully to be impenetrable to the average person?

How could I tell you in a way that you would believe?

What if I told you of Wachovia, a North-Carolina-based major bank, which settled a case with the U.S. Government in 2010 admitting it laundered $343 billion worth of money from Mexican criminals into dollar accounts.

THREE HUNDRED THIRTY-FOUR BILLION dollars.

That amount of money is equal to ONE THIRD of the Gross Domestic Product of Mexico.

It is an amount more than TWELVE TIMES greater than the annual budget of the state government of North Carolina.

Essentially, as money became tight with the growing financial crisis, Wachovia used drug money to shore up its reserves.

It was not the first major international bank to do so. It was not the last to be caught doing so. It was not at all the largest bank to be caught doing so.

The money entered into the banking system in Mexico. After being laundered by Wachovia, it sometimes exited on the other end as payments to airplane brokers and yacht brokers. Some of the intercontinental business jets purchased with the money were later captured by the U.S. Government smuggling drugs into our country.

Because Wachovia went broke in the financial crisis of 2008, its assets were swallowed up (under a deal brokered by the U.S. Government) by Wells Fargo. Wells Fargo had no financial interest in covering up Wachovia's misdeeds. So it co-operated with the U.S. Government's investigation of the money-laundering activities.

When the Wachovia charges were settled in a Miami district court in 2010, Wells Fargo was forced to pay a fine and forfeitures of $160 million. This was an inconsequential amount of money for the bank.

No individuals were ever prosecuted.

There. Is that clear enough language for you? Is that language you can understand? Is that language you want to understand?

Or are you already forgetting it?

Have you already moved on?

Would you rather we talked about how beautiful Chaqueena was in a string bikini? She was wearing it when Bass and his charter party pulled up to Deuteronomy Jackson's private island in Deuteronomy's brand new mega-yacht.

Why not? Chaqueena is much more real than all those hundreds of billions of dollars. And much more interesting.

22

"You know I didn't even pay nothing for that son of a bitch," Deuteronomy said to Chaqueena. They were watching from the veranda of the island house as the yacht anchored offshore.

"Liquidated damages," he said, chuckling. "Stupid sons of bitches signed a contract with liquidated damages. Owed me thirty-thousand dollars for every day it was late. And then the economy is booming so much they take more orders for mega-yachts than they can build. Couldn't even get the parts for them. Couldn't get the engines. Couldn't get the radars. Couldn't get the mahogany. Couldn't get the motherfucking ice makers.

"Sonbitches ended up owing me the full cost of a hundred-and-forty-eight-foot, custom-built yacht. And half-a-million dollars more. I sued their asses and settled for getting the boat for free.

"Whatcha think of that baby?"

"Why you always talking about money?" Chaqueena said. "You know I don't like it. That don't make you no big man."

Deuteronomy chuckled and watched the crew on his mega-yacht complete the anchoring drill. The crew began launching the tenders and jet-skis.

"The thing is," he said, "I was going to use that boat to launder twelve million dollars out of Mexico. So there I was stuck, looking for some way to move that money home, cause I ended up getting the yacht for free. Then along came these two broke-ass crackers. Shit, that Tony Jones on the fucking bank board himself."

"You awful," Chaqueena said. "You know that."

"I'm one awful motherfucker," Deuteronomy said.

"You making me horny," Chaqueena said.

"You best let me do some awful motherfucking things to you, then," Deuteronomy said.

"You a terrible man."

"Why don't you suck on this for a little bit?"

"I ain't sucking that thing," Chaqueena said, pulling off the top of her string bikini and unleashing a beautiful pair of natural breasts that defied imagination. "It time for you to do some eating," Chaqueena said.

She strode to a lounge chair within distant view of the yacht offshore, and she reclined. Deuteronomy turned his full attention to her.

23

"Oh my God!" Gray said. "Our host is busy."

Gray handed the pair of binoculars to Bass. The two were standing in the salon of the yacht. Lancelot stood several paces aft of them.

The captain was directing the anchoring and launching of tenders from the fly bridge one story above them.

Bass looked through the binoculars. "Holy shit!" he said. He passed the binoculars, and then he glanced self-consciously at Lancelot. Lancelot was smiling

"My Lord," Gray said.

At that moment, Jessica and Lorenzo stepped inside the salon. Bass and Gray tried to distract Jessica's attention from what they were watching.

They immediately failed. Jessica could see enough without binoculars to know what was going on.

"Mmm. Mmm." She shook her head.

Lancelot let loose a snicker.

"Perhaps we should retire to the aft deck," Bass said.

"Don't do it for his sake," Jessica said. "He wants you to be watching. He's putting on a show."

Bass herded the party toward the aft deck.

Off their stern, spread over an area of a couple of square miles, in water so spectacularly turquoise it was irridescent, stretched a flotilla of some three-dozen mega-yachts, ringed by low cliffs, tropical forest, and brilliant, white beaches. Jet-skis and sport boats screamed between and around the enormous yachts.

"We came to the absolute middle of nowhere, Bass said, "And this is where the mega-rich gather to go swimming."

"They all want to buy their own island in the Exumas," Jessica said. "Johnny Depp, Oprah, David Copperfield. John Malone. It's the thing, now. There's an Arab prince rumored to be buying the biggest deal yet."

Deuteronomy's yacht was far from the largest in the flotilla. One yacht was close to the size of a cruise ship. It was anchored farther out than the others, constrained by its draft from coming closer to shore. Several garage-size bays were open along its waterline, and a string of sport boats, jet-skis, sailboats, and paddle boards bobbed behind it.

Some of the boats had inflatable watersides deployed from their highest decks down to the crystal water alongside. The children of the super-rich slid down these water slides, squealing with glee. They congregated in the water below, swam back to the yachts, and did it again.

Security guards watched them from the decks.

Bass's cell phone rang. He stepped away from the others for a brief conversation.

"Tony's pilot doesn't want to land the Lear at Staniel Cay," he reported to the others. "The runway's too rough. A plane lost a wheel there last week. They're diverting to Black Point, five miles south of here. We can run down in one of the speed boats to pick them up."

24

I just reread that last scene, and I don't really believe it. I've seen that gathering of mega-yachts myself in Big Major's Spot near Staniel Cay. I've seen it in reality, with my own eyes, in May of the year, at the height of their seasonal migration to that part of the world.

I'm not quite sure why I don't believe it when I read it in a novel.

Maybe I don't really want to believe it.

These italicized interruptions might begin to irritate, I realize.

"Get back to work," you're probably thinking. "Get out of the story. Just tell it, and make us forget about you!"

25

The twelve-year-old girl leaned against Portia. Portia could smell the home life on her. Fried food. Cigarette smoke. Staleness. The girl was tall for her age and obese. Her clothes were worn. Her breasts were beginning to form, stretching against her too-tight tee-shirt.

Portia stroked her hair. The child put her arm around Portia.

"What do you need, darling?" Portia said.

"Miz Stephens! Miz Stephens! Miz Stephens!" a little boy said insistently, jumping up and down some ten feet away.

The girl stood on her toes to whisper in Portia's ear. "I got blood in my panties," she said.

"Miz Stephens! Miz Stephens! Miz Stephens!" the little boy continued.

"Just a moment, Tyrone," Portia said. To the little girl: "I can help you with that."

"Miz Stephens! Miz Stephens! Miz Stephens!"

"What, Tyrone?" Portia said.

"Miz Stephens! You got any crack heads in your neighborhood?" the little boy said.

"Why do you ask that, Tyrone?" Portia said.

"You know what a crack head is- They walking around all: 'Whoaa...'" Tyrone rolled his eyes back in his head and stumbled aimlessly.

Portia laughed a bit. "Oh yes," she said. "I may have seen some people like that."

"Crack heads!" Tyrone repeated, and he imitated a crack head once again for the class, drawing laughter.

"Tyrone," Portia said, beckoning the boy to come closer, "I'm going to need your help. I'm going to need you to go to Mrs. Rodriguez and ask her to come here."

"She got her period, ain't she?" Tyrone said. "She bleeding out her whoo-whoo." Tyrone danced in front of the class, pointing towards his crotch.

The girl struck like a cobra.

"Motherfucker!" she snarled. She grabbed Tyrone by his dreadlocks, snatched his head back, and landed three or four good punches to his face before Portia could pull her off.

The class sprang to their feet, squealing and shouting.

Blood spurted from Tyrone's nose. He staggered against the white board, too stunned to fight back.

Portia hugged the girl and herded her to the opposite side of the teacher's desk.

"Marina," Portia said to a quiet girl at the front of the class, "push the red button."

Marina knew immediately what to do. She went to the wall and pushed a large red button on a switch box.

Tyrone was crying. Blood was pooling on the floor. The class was still on their feet, shouting as if they were at a prize fight.

Within one minute, a policeman and an assistant principal arrived. The class immediately silenced themselves and sat down. Portia calmed the girl combatant and was able to lead her by the hand to the assistant principal. The policeman pulled a handkerchief from his pocket and began to care for Tyrone.

Within a month, Portia wouldn't be able to remember this incident as distinct from any other classroom incident that year, or the previous year, or any of the past dozen years she had worked at this place.

She and the class went on with their day, as Tyrone and his assailant were processed through the school nurse's office and the school disciplinary process.

Portia taught the class about democracy. It would be on their standardized test later that week.

26

Bass, Lancelot, Jessica, and Lorenzo rode in the speedboat to Black Point. The tiny Bahamian settlement was in a beautiful setting, but it was shabby and poor. A driver took them to the airport- an airstrip with a small building for customs inspections.

The customs agents on duty glowered suspiciously at Lancelot as the group entered the building. Lancelot avoided eye contact.

Tony was walking from his plane. The co-pilot was pulling Tony's luggage behind.

Tony seemed surprised to see Jessica.

"You remember Jessica," Bass said.

"Certainly," said Tony. "I didn't know your father was bringing you. What a delight to see you again."

"My father doesn't know I'm here," Jessica said.

There was a silence.

"Jessica and I are married," Lorenzo said.

"And my father doesn't know yet," Jessica said. "He doesn't know I'm here. He doesn't know I'm married, and he doesn't know Lorenzo. That's about the gist of it."

As they walked to the waiting pickup truck, Tony's face was cloudy.

In the truck, Tony spoke, "Listen, Jessica. You're a banker. You can get where I'm coming from. Bass and I are involved in a pretty substantial business deal with your father. I'm not sure I want to be in this situation."

"I understand exactly where you're coming from," Jessica said. "But frankly, I assumed you had discussed this with your brother when he invited me."

Lorenzo said, "Bass invited me."

"And your wife wasn't included?" Jessica said, turning to her husband.

"She certainly was," Bass said. "And my brother is being a pig."

"I'm not being a pig," Tony said. "Jessica's a big girl. She knows how this works."

They didn't speak for a while as the truck drove the mile or two back to the town dock.

"Well, it's done," Jessica said. "He's my father. If he's got a problem with me, it won't be the first time. I won't let him drag you two into it. I promise you that."

The mate drove the boat back to Deuteronomy's private island via the Exuma Sound. The water was a thousand feet deep here and sparklingly dark- a brilliant, sapphire blue. It was a spectacular ride. Surf broke against the rocky shores of the half-a-dozen beautiful islands they passed. Luxury houses lay widely scattered on the hilltops.

Tony got sick to his stomach.

He was determined not to let the others know it.

Lancelot threw up lustily over the gunwale.

27

The dinner that evening in Deuteronomy's island home went as badly as Tony expected.

Deuteronomy was furious at his daughter's presence. He was even more furious with her marriage. He glared at Lorenzo. Deuteronomy didn't speak to him all evening.

They were in an open-air dining room offering moonlit views of the islands, the sea, and the flotilla of yachts anchored in the bay. Deuteronomy's chef served an elegant meal. Expensive wine and cognac flowed. A tropical breeze cooled them.

Chaqueena wore a tight-fitting, macramé dress and platform heels. She kissed Tony on the cheek when he arrived.

Tony and Deuteronomy both felt the usual need to compete in such a setting.

Tony had no vacation home as nice as this. His place on Figure Eight Island in North Carolina was larger, perhaps, but it was not situated on its own, private island. And the setting was nowhere near as spectacular. Neither did he have the mega yacht to go with it.

Everyone knew Tony enjoyed far greater status among business elite of their city back home. He belonged to the right clubs. He had the right friends. He had the right access.

Tony and Deuteronomy both laughed loudly and uproariously at each other's funny stories.

Jessica was effectively silenced for this meal by her father's disapproval and rage. Lorenzo had nothing to say.

Bass and Gray drank too much, were far too much at ease, said things to show they couldn't care less about the two rich men's battle of egos.

Lancelot had been sent to dine on the yacht with the crew.

As the party was breaking up, Tony and Deuteronomy stood on the veranda. Deuteronomy pointed out the islands around them, dropping the names of famous people who owned them.

"And up there," he said, sweeping his hand to the north, "that's the national park."

"I've read about that," Tony said.

"Plenty of places you can go up there, ain't nobody in sight but you. You got the whole beautiful beach all to yourself."

"You've got an impressive setup here, Deuteronomy," Tony said, with a condescending tone.

"I tell you what," Deuteronomy said. "I got some work I gotta take care of in the morning. You need to let Chaqueena take you up there. She's a good boat driver. She knows all the secret places up there.

"Chaqueena, honey," he said, beckoning. He wrapped his arm around her and held her too close. "Why don't you take Tony up to the park tomorrow morning? Show him our special beach?"

"You don't get seasick, do you Tony?" Chaqueena said, smiling.

Tony felt an aching in his balls.

28

Chaqueena was driving a beat-up Boston Whaler powered by an even more beat-up outboard. But she drove it expertly.

Her yellow bikini was covered with an old-fashioned, sleeveless t-shirt. The effect was highly distracting. There was a lot of wiggling.

The guests on the yacht were seated at the outdoor dining table when Chaqueena stepped on board. Chaqueena and Jessica did not acknowledge each other.

"You ready to go to the beach, Tony?" Chaqueena asked.

The men could not find their voices.

Tony leaped from his chair. "I need a hat," he said, rubbing his bald spot.

"Well, you better get it," Chaqueena said. She was wearing no hat. Her sunglass lenses were the size of saucers. The frames were bright red.

Tony retrieved a ball cap from below. The two climbed in the Whaler and sped away from the anchorage.

Chaqueena took a winding route through the most beautiful islets, reefs, rocks, and mangrove thickets. She kept to the sheltered water. Tony, who had been terrified that he would be seasick, was relieved.

The wind blew the wife-beater t-shirt tight against her. Her string bikini offered little support as the boat bounced in the chop.

"You've done this before," Tony shouted against the wind. He held on to the console with one hand and his hat with the other.

"Deuteronomy love me to take him out to the beach," Chaqueena said.

Tony was aware that he was becoming aroused. His swim trunks would soon betray this arousal. He willed the opposite.

"You know _____ _____?" Chaqueena asked. She pointed toward a small island with a lovely home cantilevered on a sea-cliff.

"I didn't catch the name," Tony said. When she repeated it, it was no help.

"The NBA star!" Chaqueena said.

Tony shrugged.

"Well that his house," Chaqueena said. "We go over there all the time. He ain't here this week, though."

She wheeled the boat through a narrow, twisting channel that led to an open area. Larger islands stretched ahead of them. There were fewer buildings visible.

The water grew rougher.

"You better sit beside me," Chaqueena said, patting the small bench seat behind the console.

Tony sat, but this required him to lean against Chaqueena, and the mental struggle against the natural process occurring in his swim trunks grew more challenging.

In fifteen minutes they came to a stop off a pink-sand beach.

No houses were in sight. No boats were in sight. Nothing but sea and island and forest. Rocks, sand, and birds. The water underneath the boat was transparent.

Chaqueena went to the bow and dropped an anchor.

"Nobody's here," she said. "And there probably won't be any-body here. We never see anybody else here."

Tony remained seated. Tony Jones never blushed. He won-dered if he was blushing now.

"Tony," Chaqueena said, "I like to go skinny dipping when I come here. I don't know about you. It's not going to embarrass you, is it?"

"Not in the least," Tony said.

Chaqueena turned her back to him and pulled the flimsy t-shirt over her head. The bikini, top and bottom, came off next. She stepped up on the bow of the boat, balanced for a moment, turned to Tony and said, "Come on, let's swim to the beach."

She dove into the water.

Tony stripped off his bathing suit, wrestling a bit with his arousal. He dove into the water behind her. She had nearly swum to the beach by then.

29

Bass and Gray had come ashore on Deuteronomy's island with snorkeling gear and fishing spears. The captain had given them directions to a sea cave where he said they could shoot a grouper.

Their shoes were inadequate for the sharp Bahamian rock. They proceeded in fits and starts through the manchioneel bushes, circling a low promontory, wincing as the rocks hurt their feet.

As they picked their way around the cliff face, they found Deuteronomy no more than forty feet away. He was seated on a wooden bench facing the sea, smoking an enormous joint.

"Gentlemen!" he said, as soon as he noticed them. "You've come to shoot my fish!"

Neither man knew what to say.

"The captain sent you, I bet," Deuteronomy said. He took an enormous hit off the joint, blew the smoke out through his nostrils, and held the joint out toward them.

"It will blow your mind," he said.

Bass and Gray hurried toward him.

By the time they had finished, Bass and Gray were very mellow.

"Dude," Gray said. "I gotta like sit down."

"Sit down, my man," said Deuteronomy, sliding over to make room. "Sit and enjoy the view."

Both men sat with him . They looked over the maze of small islands and reefs Tony and Chaqueena had just driven through on the Whaler. The sun was higher now. The colors of the reefs and the sea cliffs were astonishing.

"I could sit here all day," said Deuteronomy.

"What a fucking place, man," said Gray.

30

Jessica's bathing suit was nothing like Chaqueena's. It was a one-piece, solid blue, like something you'd see on the beach at Figure Eight Island. Jessica was near thirty, and, while she was an attractive woman in a business suit, her life as an investment banker had left her with the figure of an office worker.

Lorenzo was no more enthusiastic about putting his own pasty body in swim trunks.

But they were married, and young, and in love. They had had sex four times already since they had been on the yacht, and they had fought three times, wrestling to keep their voices low so the others on the yacht wouldn't hear.

Jessica took a seat behind Lorenzo on the jet-ski, clasped her arms comfortably around his waist, and kissed his neck.

Lorenzo tried to start the jet-ski, but he fudged it, flinging himself and Jessica off the machine. The jet-ski stopped immediately.

They climbed back on board. The mate swam out to meet them and give them another word of instruction.

This time it went better. Lorenzo spun them quickly around the perimeter of the yacht flotilla, and the two sped out of sight around the north point of the island.

31

"What you want to shoot my fish for?" Deuteronomy asked his two companions.

"Hey, we aren't killers man," Gray said. "We like your fish."

"Pay him no mind, Deuteronomy," Bass said.

"Hey," Gray said, "how the hell do you know those are your fish? They live in the ocean. They could have swum over here from anywhere."

"But they're here at his island, Gray," Bass said, trying to rein his friend in. "And he's nice enough to be chartering his boat to us."

"I'm just saying," Gray said. And he drifted off into his buzz.

"Wonder what your brother's doing?" Deuteronomy asked.

The others did not answer.

"Bass," Deuteronomy said, "you didn't have any trouble making those transfers I recommended?"

"It all went right through. Just like you said," Bass said.

"What transfers?" Gray asked.

"Gray! Damnit!" Bass said.

"We just moving a little money around," Deuteronomy said.

"You aren't moving money," Gray said. "You're just moving imaginary bullshit."

"Gray," Bass said, "would you..."

"I mean think about it," Gray continued. "It doesn't fucking exist. It's just numbers in cyberspace. Pure imagination."

Bass said, "You've just got to ignore him."

"No. Don't do that to me," Gray said. "I'm serious. I mean I get so fucking tired of hearing about money. You're just moving imaginary numbers around in cyberspace. It's not like you're moving around suitcases full of cash."

There was a silence here. The waves splashed gently against the rocks in front of them.

"And even if it was cash," Gray continued, "and I know perfectly well it wasn't. But if it was fucking steamer trunks full of cash, what the hell is that but imaginary numbers printed on slips of paper? I mean face it. It's not real. You can't eat it. You can't fuck it. It's just nothing but your imagination printed on a piece of paper, and people let it get them so worked up they'll..."

Bass stood up suddenly and started pacing.

"Gray," he said, "Let's go fishing."

"Why are you trying to shut me up?" Gray said. "I'm just catching a buzz with my bro here and talking some trash. Hey, Deuteronomy. I mean it looks like you might actually have some money, man." He waved his arm unsteadily at the island around him. "At least it's not just a bunch of bullshit, like Tony Jones. Tony Jones ain't got any money. He's just got imaginary numbers. And most of it is imaginary numbers that he owes other people."

"Deuteronomy," Bass said, "I apologize for my stoned friend."

Deuteronomy waved his complaint away.

Gray could not be stopped. "What's Tony Jones's creed?" Gray said.

Bass arched his eyebrows at him in desperation. Gray took no notice.

"What does Tony Jones always tell us his creed is? The Entrepreneur's Creed he calls it."

Bass said nothing. He looked despondent.

"The Entrepreneur's Creed," Gray continued. "Did you ever hear that Deuteronomy? Hey, you're an entrepreneur. It's great. What is it? 'A dollar borrowed is a dollar earned.'"

Bass suffered in silence.

"'A dollar borrowed is a dollar earned," Gray repeated.

Deuteronomy scowled.

"A dollar refinanced is a dollar saved," Gray continued. He chuckled to himself.

He paused for effect.

"And a dollar repaid is lost forever." Gray guffawed. "A dollar repaid is lost forever. This is Charlotte's leading real estate magnate. And that's his fucking creed. How many times has he told us that, Bass?"

Bass said nothing.

"Sombitch is on the fucking bank board," Gray continued. "He's the guy in charge of watching out for all the poor fuckers' imaginary money. Jesus Christ."

Deuteronomy chuckled softly.

"So that's what I'm telling you my man," Gray continued. "It's all just make-believe. It ain't real."

"That's not how my brother really operates," Bass said. "You know that."

"You two fuckers get the hell off my island," Deuteronomy said.

32

Chaqueena emerged from the transparent sea. Streaming. Buxom. Callipygian. Cinnamon. She strode across the pink sand.

Tony emerged from the water several paces behind her.

She laughed.

"I think you like skinny-dipping, Tony," she said, smiling at his tumescence.

Tony grinned like an idiot. He hurried toward her.

She walked along the shoreline.

Tony caught up and walked beside her.

"Don't it feel great between your toes?" she said. "It ain't like nothing else I ever felt." She squished her toes in the wet, pink sand. They disappeared into it and reappeared. Disappeared. Reemerged.

Tony was speechless.

She laughed. "Deuteronomy say it's like walking in a giant pussy."

She swerved toward the water's edge and walked there, splashing lightly.

Tony took her in his arms and tried to kiss her.

"Oh Tony," she said, smiling and eluding his grasp. "You can't do that."

Tony stood naked, turgid, bewildered.

"Tony, darling," Chaqueena said, with a chastising expression, "you better not lay a hand on me. Deuteronomy will cut your balls off if he catches you."

She turned and continued walking down the beach.

Tony heard the whining of a jet-ski coming around the point.

Chaqueena stopped. "Ooh! Somebody's coming! Quick, run!"

She sprinted down the beach past him. He ran like a madman after her.

33

"Gray, you can't shut up, can you?" Bass said, as the launch backed away from Deuteronomy's dock.

"If you ask me, that dude's got a short fuse," Gray said.

Lancelot laughed heartily.

"And a couple of screws loose," Gray said.

"That's the man," Lancelot said. "That's the man."

"All the hell I did was talk about money," Gray said. "And I wasn't even talking about his money. I was just stoned and saying some shit. Shit I happen to really believe about money. And all of a sudden he goes all serial killer on me."

"You were saying some outrageous things about my brother," Bass said.

"They weren't true? Are you telling me you haven't heard Tony say exactly that? He's been saying that as long as I've known him."

"You just don't know what's going on."

"You're right. I don't have any idea what's going on. You invite me on a boat trip. We've got to stop in and visit the biggest thug in Charlotte. There's some secret thing going on. Now you're chewing me out about it."

"What did the man say?" Lancelot said.

"He just told us to get the fuck off his island," Gray said. "Then we see him get on a jet-ski and speed off by himself."

"That fucker crazy," Lancelot said. "You two ought to get on that yacht and get the hell out of here."

34

Tony dove into the water behind Chaqueena and swam toward the boat. She disappeared beneath the surface and came up on the far side. Chaqueena peeked behind the stern at the jet-ski coming into view.

"Aw hell," she said. "It's just his daughter and that pasty-ass fucker she married."

Chaqueena grabbed the upper casing of the outboard and hauled herself out of the water. She waved to the approaching jet-ski.

She walked to the bow, picked up her bathing suit pieces, and stepped into the bottoms, snapping the elastic strings around her hips.

Tony cowered behind the boat.

"You want your bathing suit, Tony?" Chaqueena said. She picked up his suit, making no effort to be discreet, and tossed it over the side to him.

She put her top on backward, tied it over her stomach, and spun it around to slide over her breasts. She lifted her breasts with the string she tied behind her neck.

The jet-ski stopped some hundred yards away, near the beach.

"They ain't being real sociable," Chaqueena said. "Maybe they come up here to get some."

Tony said nothing.

"Why don't you climb on up in the boat, Tony? We best get on back. I don't want Deuteronomy to think you were up here trying to fuck me."

Tony tried climbing up the outboard motor as she had done. He couldn't pull himself out of the water.

"Here," Chaqueena said. She flipped a swim ladder over the stern of the boat.

Tony could climb that.

Jessica and Lorenzo were standing on the beach now.

"What the hell she staring at?" Chaqueena said. "I can't stand that Harvard MBA motherfucker."

Chaqueena stomped to the bow of the whaler and began pulling in the anchor line. She raised the anchor and went back to start the engine.

She drove the boat toward the jet-ski and turned the outboard off.

"Where your daddy?" she said.

"I don't know," Jessica said.

"He told me to bring Tony up here," Chaqueena said.

"Well I can see you did," Jessica said.

"You ain't gotta get a attitude about it," Chaqueena said.

"What kind of an attitude do you think I have?" Jessica said.

"Don't you get all Harvard with me, missy."

"I'm sorry?"

"Come up in here on your daddy goddamn yacht and act like you too good for this shit."

"Well, who's got an attitude now? You enjoy your skinny-dip, Tony?" Jessica asked.

Tony was momentarily speechless. Then he blurted out, "Harvard Business?"

"Yes," Jessica said. "I see you at the alumni meetings in Charlotte."

"Oh, you in the goddamn club together," Chaqueena said. "That Tony love skinny-dipping. You ought to see him."

"I imagine he does," Jessica said.

The two women stared at each other across the shallow, crystalline water.

The buzz of another jet-ski approached from behind the point.

35

When Deuteronomy brought his jet-ski to a stop, he held on to the side of the side of the runabout. Chaqueena avoided his eyes.

"It's a family reunion up here," he said.

No one responded.

"My daughter. My son." His voice was acid with sarcasm. "My..." He looked Chaqueena up and down.

"She something else, ain't she Tony?" Deuteronomy said. "You ever seen anything like that?"

"She's a gracious hostess," Tony said.

"Gracious?" Deuteronomy said. He laughed. "I bet she was. You keep your clothes on, Honey?"

Chaqueena said nothing.

"She love to take those clothes off," Deuteronomy said. "She a professional. Come on over here, honey."

Chaqueena came to his side of the boat. Deuteronomy grabbed her butt cheek in his hand. "Get your ass on over here. I'm liable to take those little clothes off right here. Can't help myself."

Chaqueena swatted playfully at his hand.

Deuteronomy slid his hand underneath the string bikini.

"Tony," Deuteronomy said. "Why don't you take this jet-ski back and let me stay here with Chaqueena? I got some bidness I need to take care of."

"I don't have to take this," Jessica said.

"Tony," Deuteronomy said. "A man got to take care of a woman like this. Got to watch her like his money. Everybody be trying to grab some of it if he don't watch out."

Deuteronomy stepped into the boat.

Tony climbed out of the boat and onto the jet-ski. Deuteronomy grabbed Chaqueena's butt with both hands and gave her a passionate, open-mouthed kiss.

Deuteronomy shouted toward Lorenzo. "Son-in-law, stick around, I'll show you how the old man do it."

Lorenzo and Jessica climbed on their jet-ski.

Tony followed them zipping out of the cove. Lorenzo and Jessica didn't look back. But Tony couldn't help himself. Deuteronomy was standing naked in the bow section of the runabout, one hand behind him, bracing against the console. Chaqueena was on her knees before him.

Tony watched only a moment. Then he, too, zipped out of sight behind the point and sped toward the chartered yacht.

36

Tony was flying home from the yachting trip when his first exit deal began to go bad. He was supposed to be selling a twenty-five story office building in downtown Charlotte. Tony and his partners had bought the building from the insurance company (now defunct) that originally built it. Tony renovated it into some of the highest-quality space downtown. He filled it with prime tenants on solid leases and contracted to sell it to a Real Estate Investment Trust.

It was a solid deal. Tony Jones was a solid businessman. There was nothing edgy about it.

Tony had sensed displeasure from the buyers for the past month or so. They had modeled their returns based on using heavy leverage- a lot of borrowed money- nothing unusual in the current business environment.

But lending was getting tighter. The buyers were either going to have to do the deal with less leverage, or they were going to have to pay higher interest rates than they had planned. That was going to cut into their returns. Lower returns were going to cut into their stock price, which would cut into the executives' compensation. The result: a little change in the numbers had the potential to make a big change in the personal wealth of the people running the deal.

Tony knew all this, and he couldn't have cared less. The sales contract was ironclad. He and his partners were going to get out clean in a falling market. The other guys would catch the falling knife. Tough shit. That was business.

But these guys didn't want to catch the knife, and they had better lawyers.

The labyrinthine negotiations. The scheming. The posturing. The lying. The number crunching. The legal bills. The hours at the conference tables. The hours on the phones. The hours over breakfast, lunch, dinner. The bottles of wine. The bottles of expensive water. The single-malt Scotches. The martinis. The pretentious choices from the menus. The more pretentious special orders. The phone calls not returned. The feigned disinterest. The quiet desperation. The rages. The staplers flung across the office. The threats to sue. The furious calls to the attorneys. The ups. The downs. The gyrations. The work. The sweat. The determination. The grit. The despair.

And in the end, in the very end, it was a detail on the environmental report. A finding of asbestos. One little corner Tony vaguely remembered cutting when they were upfitting the project. One little two-hundred-thousand-dollar shortcut he had signed off on. One forgotten decision on one forgotten day years ago- a decision he made only because it was a way to make a little more money, and Tony had disciplined himself all his adult life ALWAYS to make a little more money when it could be made. No one would ever have noticed it. No government inspector would ever have found it. Only some delver being paid and goaded to dig up that insignificant little skeleton in the project files stored in banker's boxes in a warehouse in North Charlotte.

The fucking bastard.

Tony would have loved to rip the little bastard's balls off, if he could have found out who the little file-grubbing bastard was.

Tony walked out of his attorney's office five weeks later, having been informed by three senior partners, who were charging him a total of two-thousand dollars an hour for the meeting, that his twenty-five-million-dollar deal was dead and gone, and there was not a thing he could do about it.

He would never find another buyer in this market, he knew. The market was going to shit. This was bad. It might be worse than anything he had ever seen.

37

Bass had neglected to tell Portia of Tony's loan from Deuteronomy. As far as Portia knew, Bass and Tony had both inherited substantial shares of their mother's Texas oil money.

When her attorneys did the check on Bass's accounts, they found what they expected to find. She had not paid particular attention to this. She really treated the entire affair something like an HIV test for her fiancé. She just had to get it over with. She really didn't want to know any details.

The financial report came back fine. All that was missing was the Figure Eight house, and, her attorneys informed her, she could perfectly well shop for and decorate this home along with her fiancé as if it were going to be hers. The home would have to be held as joint property after they were married. That was in the will.

Portia was so sick and tired of that stupid will, and now she had a fiancé who didn't need to worry about her stupid money, the money she couldn't touch and didn't really give a damn about. Maybe there was some wisdom in the way her father set it all up.

She loved her father so. She missed him so. When Bass held her in his arms and kissed her on the forehead all she could think of was her father, and the way he had done that. Her father was a big man like Bass, a whale of a man.

Tears would come to her eyes sometimes when Bass held her. And he would ask why. And she would just shake her head and not tell him.

But he knew. He knew what she was thinking.

38

The second deal Tony Jones lost was more spectacular.

In this one, the bad guys were really, really bad.

Tony made the distinction between bad guys and good guys quite often. He often pronounced this judgment to his friends as he discussed those with whom he did business.

"He's a great guy!"

"He's a son of a bitch. A real bad guy."

Bass had often remarked how comfortably Tony split humanity into bad guys and good guys. It amused Bass.

A good guy could become a bad guy very quickly in Tony's world. And the great guys who were under contract to buy his multi-purpose development in Davidson, North Carolina suddenly became the very, very bad guys who were backing out of the deal.

They didn't come up with a legal way out as the first guys did. These newly minted bad guys just informed Tony they weren't going to be able to close, and they were walking away.

"The whole world has blown up," their guy told Tony over a dinner in Atlanta. The dinner was fine. It was expensive. The atmosphere was great. Nothing appeared to be blowing up where they were eating their steaks and drinking their expensive wine.

"What the fuck do you mean the whole world has blown up?" Tony shouted. People in the restaurant turned to look. "Don't tell me about the world blowing up, you son of a bitch. I'm perfectly goddamned aware of what is going on in financial markets, and that, I will remind you, does not invalidate the goddamned contract we have."

At this point in the financial meltdown, some people in the restaurant were still a bit astonished at this scene. But the more active business people in the audience just raised their eyebrows at each other or shook their heads in distaste. Then they turned back to their dinner.

"I don't have to take this," the now-bad guy said to Tony.

"You know what?" Tony said loudly, jabbing his finger toward the bad guy. "You're dead wrong about that. You're going to have to take it. And you're going to have to take the triple damages lawsuit I slap on your ass tomorrow. Triple damages. That's ninety-goddamn-million dollars, asshole! Ninety-million dollars!"

The bad guy stood up, red in the face. He threw his cloth napkin into the middle of his plate of food.

"Boy," he said. "Everything they say about Tony Jones is true. Go on and waste your money on lawyers, asshole. They're going to be standing in a long line."

And the bad guy just walked away from the table, as half the restaurant stared at him.

"Goddamn," Tony said to himself. He sat and stared. "Goddamn."

39

Nerissa was the hostess of Portia's bachelorette party. A good deal of drinking and pretending to be naughty went on.

None of the women really intended to be very naughty.

They were, after all, celebrating an impending wedding- a commitment on the part of their guest of honor to remain sexually faithful to one man. These women were devoted romantics.

Let's face it, they all wanted love. They wanted love beyond reasonable hope, perhaps. But they had the clearest concept of this love. They had the clearest, most insatiable drive to obtain it.

Not one of them could define love satisfactorily.

But each of them (as do you) knew immediately what it meant.

This is what they wanted.

And this is what they believed marriage could supply their friend (and them, too.)

Let's shift now, to the part of the evening where they had too much to drink. It was a bit after midnight. They called a cab. They put tiaras on their heads and a sash over Portia's shoulder identifying her as the bride-to-be. They directed the cab driver to take them to their favorite night club.

When they arrived, they entered loudly, proclaiming their status as bachelorettes.

And lo, who was at this night spot but Bass, and his friend Gray, and their friend Lorenzo?

Jessica was among the bachelorette party celebrants. She went immediately to her husband and kissed him coyly.

The other "bachelorettes" thought this was "cute." They all wished they could be this married and this much in love. Even those who were already married aspired to this ideal, as different as it might be from their own realities.

The bachelorette of honor went immediately to the arms of her fiancé. And while she was drunk, and she got drunker, and she didn't particularly behave very well the rest of the evening, she remained loyally at his side until she went home.

This left Gray without a girl. But Gray was connected enough with the group to be drawn into the midst of the festivities.

They danced drunkenly and drank shots of sickeningly sweet liqueur and made themselves the rowdy center of attention for another hour or two.

At some point, very late in the early morning hours, as the party had begun to break up, Portia noticed Nerissa was missing. Some time later, she noticed Gray was missing. But she gave this only a fleeting thought.

That thought contained an irrational longing for that indefinable thing they all hoped for. She wanted love for Nerissa, she drunkenly and fleetingly thought. And she wanted love for Gray, she drunkenly and fleetingly thought.

The next morning found Nerissa naked in bed in Gray's apartment, still a bit drunk, already very hung over. She looked up to see Gray climb naked out of the bed and sheepishly head toward the bathroom. When Nerissa remembered (with some horror) the hour and fifteen minutes of sexual acrobatics she had performed with this man in the pre-dawn hours, the entire scene, you see- the entire scene had in some way been set up by Portia's fleeting prayer some hours before.

What but that irrational yearning for love, that indefinable thing that lies beyond hope, had caused this outcome? What else propels our story, in the end? What else moves it all along?

40

Tony Jones was not in trouble. He was far from it, in fact.

His business continued in fine fashion. By the end of the summer, development deals were drying up all over the country. Developers were going broke. Bankers were losing their jobs. People were beginning to act in desperate ways.

Tony had to lay off several of his junior development partners. He just couldn't see cash flow to support their salaries in this market. But he himself was in no danger. He had seen the crash approaching, had cut back on his development expenditures, and had few deals in the pipeline.

And his biggest sale was still out there. Tony crowed to himself privately that he was going to come through this recession with forty million dollars in solid cash reserves, not to mention the money he had salted away in Bass's overseas accounts in T-bills. Sure, he owed that money back to Deuteronomy Jackson, but with as much liquidity as Tony expected to have, he was thinking he might just roll over the loan- to prove he was one of the only people who could do it in this environment.

Plus, Tony knew, his brother was about to become a bloody billionaire. Bass would surely look to Tony to handle his business affairs.

It was a perfect storm of good luck, Tony reasoned. He was going to be one of the most liquid real estate developers in the country, at a time when everybody was going bust. There would be deals to be had in any market- at fire-sale prices.

This might be the moment that made his career, Tony thought. He could become the next Sam Zell. The next Alfred Taubman. The name Trump crossed his mind momentarily, but Trump was such a joke. Tony, unlike Trump, would be solid and low-key. He probably already had more money than Trump, he knew. Tony, like any of the real developers he admired, would keep his name out of the tabloids. He would be a real mover and shaker. He thought of the idiot Trump on T.V. Tony had flipped past Trump's show once and watched for a couple of minutes. Jesus, he laughed.

Tony imagined what it would be like to be a real billionaire. To have real, fuck-you money. Even if it was predominately his brother's money. They would be a powerhouse. He wouldn't care what anyone thought. He would dictate the terms. The deals would come to him. The women would come to him.

Chaqueena would come to him. He would take her away from the psychopath Jackson. He would screw her in his Maserati. He imagined how they would work her legs around the gear shift.

Tony chuckled out loud to himself.

"Hell," he said. "That bitch is crazier than he is."

41

As Labor Day of 2008 came and went, and as Tony Jones continued his dreams, Jessica White found herself in a terrible bind.

The recession was beginning to be felt on her floor at the office. Investment bankers were losing their jobs. The ones who were being let go were not moving on to other banks and other high-paying jobs. The market was drying up.

People weren't just losing their jobs. They were losing their careers.

What were they going to do? They were people who made six- and seven-figure bonuses. Now they were at home with nothing to do. No income. No real prospects.

Jessica knew real people like this.

She did her best to avoid contact with them, as close as she might have been with them in the past. She found reasons not to respond to their phone calls or their emails. It was just too depressing. She couldn't do anything to help them. If she didn't talk to them or correspond with them, she didn't think about them as much. That felt better.

Still, she knew she was in danger.

She was working on a mortgage-backed securities deal. The syndication had been rather hastily thrown together, she knew. Her team leader explained they were trying to get this one in under the wire. No one was sure how much longer these deals could be marketed, but management wanted it done. They put together a crack team to get the bonds issued and sold while there was still time.

The bonds had been rated by Standard and Poors. The tranches were laid out. The securitization agreements, voluminous and expensive, had been prepared by outside law firms.

Now it was the salespeople's turn to work their magic. Jessica and her team were to place two-hundred-million dollars in mortgage-backed bonds the first week of September.

The market was shaky and skittish. But there were bonuses to be earned. Big bonuses.

Jessica and her team huddled in a conference room before the sales push began.

"O.K., you fuckers," her team leader said. "You fucking animals. We've seen what's happening. We've seen these pussies getting led out of here to spend the rest of their careers working at the fucking hardware store. And you're the ones who are still here. You're the ones with the balls and the gumption to survive and prosper in this environment. You're the future of this bank. You're the future of this industry. You're the future of America. The future of very rich people in America. Now get out there and close this fucking deal and get rich!"

42

You know what? That's not the way it happened at all. That's the way you might imagine it happened. You've watched movies. But those are just fictionalizations.

Here's the way it really happened.

In the most subdued and boring tones, using language that would quickly lose your interest in this novel, terms that mean nothing to you, terms like basis points and tranches and clawbacks and seasoning and LIBOR and units and allocations... Using these and far more somniferous terms, with a flat, monotone delivery, and the most subtle of threats- threats and promises so subtle you wouldn't even have picked up on them if you happened to be watching the scene- Jessica's manager conveyed to her and her teammates that the situation was dire. They must find a way to save themselves, and they must under no circumstances convey to any of their customers the least sense that something might be amiss.

This room full of Bloomberg terminals and computer screens and phone banks came softly alive with the sound of people speaking in very hushed tones to institutional investors all over the world.

Everyone spoke as if nothing whatsoever was wrong. As if everyone involved were absolutely trustworthy. As if the integrity of their institutions, their products, the mortgages underlying those products, the homes which secured the mortgages, the Americans who owned those homes, the businesses that employed those Americans, the country that coddled and fed those businesses, the capitalist system to which they all pledged allegiance, the God who seemed to ordain it all, the whole conceptual framework in which they all existed, were stable and real and sound.

That's the way it sounded that morning in the tower high above Charlotte. That's the way it sounded later that afternoon. That's the way it sounded the next day.

And on the third day, Jessica knew it was all going to come to an end for her.

She was going to be led out of the bank carrying a pathetic, cardboard box of office mementos- to spend the rest of her career selling hardware.

43

"My darling daughter," Deuteronomy said into his cell phone.

"Are we really going to do this?" Jessica said. "Are we really going to spend our lives doing this to each other?"

There was a long silence.

"I'm sorry," Jessica said. "I truly am."

"Remarkable," her father said.

There was another awkward silence.

"I realize you're just a human being," Jessica said. "A black human being. A black man."

Deuteronomy Jackson was alone in his office now, speaking on his cell phone with his daughter.

"What the hell does that mean?" he said. His voice was a bit too deep to be convincing.

"You know what it means," Jessica said.

He said nothing.

"You know exactly what it means," Jessica said. "I haven't been fair to you. The world hasn't been fair to you."

No one was in the office to see as Deuteronomy reached to wipe his eyes.

"You did try," Jessica said. "And I want to thank you for trying."

Deuteronomy fought not to make a sound.

"There are plenty of men who don't try," Jessica continued. "I know that. You always tried, Daddy."

Jessica had not called Deuteronomy "daddy" since before she was a teenager. He took the phone down from his ear.

He put the phone back to his ear.

"My baby," he said, but he couldn't fight back the slightest sob, and she heard it. He caught himself.

"You all right," Jessica said. It was a statement. Not a question.

"You more than all right," Deuteronomy said. "You something else."

There was another silence.

"Hey listen," Jessica said. "This is a business call."

Deuteronomy welcomed the break. He got hold of himself. "What you need, baby?" he said.

"I need to sell some bonds."

44

They met at the most expensive restaurant in Charlotte. Jessica made the reservation.

She was there first. When her father arrived, she stuck out her hand. He reached out with both arms and hugged her. She put her arms around him.

After they were seated and had ordered, Jessica came clean.

"I'm going to lose my job, Daddy," she said. "I'm going to lose my job and my career in banking. I've been watching it happen to other people for nearly a year. Lots of other people. I can see the handwriting on the wall."

Deuteronomy probed. She came forward. The markets were drying up. Her usual buyers were sheepish and slow. She could feel them subtly backing away. The pressure was on from her superiors.

"Fuck em," Deuteronomy said, "It's probably time to get out. You can come to work for me. I need somebody like you baby. I need somebody to help me get into some clean shit. I don't want to be a crook the rest of my life."

Jessica was nonplussed. She had, he imagined, anticipated this. And she was handling it very, very coolly. He liked that.

"Daddy," she said, "I'm going to be straight with you. There's a business opportunity to be had here. I'm not the only one who's having trouble selling these things. So they're going to sell at a discount. The bank's going to take a bath, and they're going to be mad as hell about it, but that's just life. The thing is, these bonds are solid as hell. Basically, whoever buys them gets paid from the mortgages of hundreds of homeowners. All those homeowners aren't going to stop paying their mortgages all at once. Even if they did, then we'd just foreclose on their houses and sell them and make the bondholders whole with that. So whoever buys these things is going to end up making a hell of a lot more return than the markets usually offer. When the rest of the world gets their shit back together, I think you could unload these things at a substantial profit."

"When you say make a hell of a lot more return, what kind of money are you talking about?" Deuteronomy said.

"Bottom line?" Jessica asked. She hesitated.

"How much money can you make on this?" Deuteronomy said.

"I don't think it's unreasonable to think you might double your money in a year's time."

"This is your father you're talking to."

"This is the meanest motherfucker in Charlotte I'm talking to," said Jessica, leaning across the table and lowering her voice. "I ain't no goddamn fool."

"Well," Deuteronomy said, "what kind of bonus would you make if I bought sixty million dollars' worth of this shit?"

Jessica's couldn't quite hide her astonishment.

"Course you might have to do a little dry-cleaning on some of that money," her father said, with a fatherly smile.

45

Tom Rodham collared Deuteronomy in the lobby of the Bank of America Tower. They were both on their way upstairs for a Focus Charlotte Foundation meeting.

"Deuteronomy," Tom said, taking him gently by the elbow and leading him aside. "Have you spoken with Tony Jones lately?"

"It's been a few weeks, "Deuteronomy said.

"I've just been worried about him," Tom said. "I hear rumors. Have you heard rumors?"

"What kind of rumors?" Deuteronomy said.

"I don't want to spread anything that may not be true," Tom said.

"I know. I know," Deuteronomy said, "but Tony's a good friend of yours and a good friend of mine. I owe that dude a lot."

Tom hesitated.

"Nobody's done more for me in this town than Tony Jones," Deuteronomy said. "Tell me what you know."

"I heard he's going under," Tom said. He lowered his voice almost to a whisper. "The banks are calling everything. Big deal was supposed to close for him last week and it blew up at the closing table. It's like the third deal he's lost in a couple of months. Sure things, all of them."

Deuteronomy said nothing.

"This shit's starting to get scary," Tom said. "I mean Tony Jones..."

"He was Mr. Big," Deuteronomy said. He was cool. Very cool.

"He was kind of Mr. Charlotte in the real estate world," Tom said. "I'm just worried about Tony, and what it might be doing to him."

Deuteronomy just nodded seriously.

"I hear he's not coming today," Tom said. "I feel kind of funny calling him. I'm on the board of a bank that might be involved. But I was thinking you might give him a call and see how's he's doing. Tell him I asked about him."

"Yeh," Deuteronomy said, with a distant look. "I'll give Tony a call."

"Thanks, dude," Tom said.

"I might just stop by and see him," Deuteronomy said.

46

Dr. Ralph Burnstein had known Tony since their college days. He taught ECON 168 at Chapel Hill every fall: *Microeconomics of Real Estate Development.* This popular class filled an auditorium seating one-hundred seventy-five students. Dr. Burnstein was a respected scholar. No active real estate industry professional had ever read anything he had written, but plenty of Economics professors had.

That is not entirely accurate.

Tony Jones had read the first page of a study he paid Dr. Burnstein eighty-thousand dollars to write. The study explained how Tony's proposed mixed-use development in downtown Chapel Hill would increase economic diversity in that college town. The study had been designed (by Tony, at least) to spur the notoriously leftist zoning board to approve his project.

Tony had hired his old, left-leaning college buddy, Ralph Burnstein, to write this study. Ralph had done a yeoman's job. The Orange County planning commission had still rejected Tony's proposal out of hand.

It didn't matter in the long run. Tony found another buyer for the property before his option to purchase expired. Tony flipped the property at a small profit and kept on moving. He virtually forgot the whole episode. But Ralph remembered it.

Ralph even felt a bit of guilt over the whole thing. He emailed Tony once or twice a year, saw him at the occasional football game or basketball game in Chapel Hill, and maintained a distant camaraderie.

The previous spring, he had invited Tony to his ECON 168 class as a guest speaker in the fall of 2008.

Tony had forgotten about this. Swati started reminding him of it two weeks before the talk was due. Ralph called to remind him also, and to invite him to dine with some of their other college friends.

To top it all off, the Chancellor of the University dropped Tony a handwritten note telling him he was looking forward to the visit from a former Trustee of the University. He asked if Tony would mind if he sat in on his lecture.

All of this hit at a time when Tony Jones didn't want to do it at all. He was going broke. He was depressed. He was outraged. He was drunk. He was suicidal. He was impotent. He was completely confused. He sure as hell didn't want to talk to a goddamn college economics class about real estate development. He screamed to himself as he drove his Maserati home the evening before.

As if he fucking knew anything about real estate development!

The next day he got a ticket driving ninety-five miles an hour on I-85. He mouthed off to the cop so badly he was fortunate he didn't get yanked out of the car and beaten.

So- Tony Jones found himself at the Kenan School of Business in Chapel Hill, in an auditorium full of preppy-looking undergraduates, shaking hands with the Chancellor, and wondering why in the hell he was there.

The title of the session was "Real-World Lessons from a Mega-Developer."

Tony barely listened as Ralph gave a long-winded introduction listing the tallest, best-known office towers Tony had developed. Ralph talked with idolatrous reverence.

Tony stopped listening. He was starting to sweat. Noticeably.

The Chancellor looked like the sycophantic ass he was. Tony knew the Chancellor would hit him up for an ungodly contribution within a week. What would he do when Tony told him he was broke?

"Tony," Ralph was saying, "I don't know exactly how you want to do this, but I thought, if you're willing, we might start this off as a bit of a dialectic. The students could ask you questions. and you could talk about whatever strikes your fancy. And we'll see what learning opportunities present themselves."

"Sure, Ralph," Tony said, taking the proffered microphone. "So what exactly do you guys want to know?"

"How to make a butt load of money!" somebody shouted from back in the room. Everybody laughed. Everybody except Tony. He just grinned, and held the microphone, and thought for a long moment of silence.

"Well," Tony said, "You want to know the truth about that one?"

The classroom erupted into applause and cheers.

"Well, the truth is," Tony said, "you've basically got to steal it."

Silence.

Ralph and the Chancellor were uncomfortable.

"Hey," Tony said. "You said a butt load of money. You didn't say a return on investment. Or a living wage. Or a very comfortable wage for that matter. That's not what you're talking about. You're talking about big money. The kind of money you all dream about, but let's face it, most of you will never, ever see."

The students in the front rows were loving this, he noticed. The Chancellor actually checked his watch, as if...

"I mean we're talking, what, about hundreds of millions? About a billion dollars? I mean what exactly do you call a butt load?"

The class roared with laughter and approval. He knew he had them.

"So I'm just giving you the straight up answer," Tony said. "You gotta steal it."

"Oh Tony!" Ralph interjected.

"No," Tony said, waving Ralph away. "I'm serious. Bear with me here." He turned to the audience. "ECON, what is this, ECON 160-something?"

"One sixty-eight," Ralph said.

"You guys have had some Econ courses, right? Macro? Micro? I mean you know the basic concepts. And you know the concept of rents, right? I'm not talking rent like your apartment rent or the leases on my office buildings. I mean the Economics concept of rents, which are, what, tell me if I'm right, Ralph, returns in excess of the fair market value of a good or service?"

"Well... more or less," Ralph said.

"So what you guys want, like all good real estate developers, is to earn big rents, right?" Tony smiled, and the class roared their approval. "But we're not talking about rents like the average Joe thinks of rent. We're talking about rents like Dr. Burnstein here talks about rents. We're talking about the big bucks, the money you theoretically shouldn't be able to earn if all those graphs Dr. Burnstein projects up on the screen here were really true.

"We're not just talking about rents. We're talking about mega-rents, and let's face it," he said, "you gotta basically steal em. Because they are payments far, far in EXCESS of the fair market value."

A pretty brunette in the front row was trying to catch Tony's eye. Tony didn't miss this. She wore an impossibly short skirt.

While Tony was glancing at the brunette, the Chancellor made his move to escape. The only way out was to walk up the side aisle in front of everyone.

"Now listen," Tony said. "I'm not advocating breaking the law. At least here in public..."

The class laughed.

"What I'm saying," he continued, "is if you want to know how people make real money, it's because they've figured out how to grab more than their fair share. A whole lot more than their fair share.

"How do you steal something? Well, you can take a gun and stick it in somebody's face and make them give it to you. That works. It pisses people off, and it makes enemies, but there are rich people who've essentially made a lot of money that way.

"Not with real guns- well, I guess you've got those types, too- but I'm talking about people who trap others in situations they don't want to be in and then make them pay a whole lot of money to get out."

The class was really starting to warm to this talk.

"Or you can steal money sort of like a pickpocket does," Tony continued, "where you snatch it out of people's pockets when they aren't looking. Sort of like the bank hits your checking account up with fees. You can be so slick you steal millions or billions and people don't even really notice. They like it.

"And they LOVE you when you get rich. I mean face it, everybody in the U.S. just LOVES rich people."

They cheered and applauded. Tony was sure the brunette on the front row was spreading her legs to show him her lace thong on purpose. He was wondering if he might have time after this... when he glanced up at the Chancellor making his way out. The Chancellor had stopped. The Chancellor was glad-handing someone at the back door to the auditorium. He was adopting his most fawning, money-raising demeanor. It was a tall, black man. It was.... Deuteronomy Jackson.

How long had he been there? Deuteronomy wasn't paying attention to the Chancellor. He was glaring at Tony.

Tony lost track of what he was about to say.

There was a silence.

"Did I answer your question?" Tony said.

"Let me see if I can rephrase your answer," Ralph said, reaching to take the microphone from Tony.

The class erupted in boos and catcalls.

"I think they understood the answer, Ralph," Tony said.

The class erupted in cheers and laughter.

"Maybe we should take another question," Tony said. He gestured across the class.

"Hey, I got a question," said Deuteronomy Jackson in a commanding voice from the back. Everyone in the class turned to look at him.

"Who's the best kind of sucker to steal this money from?" Deuteronomy asked. "I mean if you're gonna steal the big bucks?"

47

Tony was not quick to reply.

Ralph reached for the microphone again, to fill the awkward silence, but Tony didn't give it to him.

"Would you mind if I invited you down here?" Tony said to Deuteronomy. "Ralph- Dr. Burnstein- do you mind? Do you know who this is?"

Ralph looked panicked and confused.

"This," Tony said to the class, waving toward Deuteronomy, "is one of the wealthiest and most successful businessmen in the state of North Carolina. He's a civic leader in Charlotte. I'm going to guess most of you have never heard of him- my good friend Deuteronomy Jackson."

Deuteronomy hesitated.

"Mr. Jackson is the largest property owner in Mecklenberg County other than Bank of America and the government. He's the number one landlord in Charlotte. I'm sorry to put you on the spot, Deuteronomy, but I think you might have a lot to teach these young people."

The Chancellor clapped loudly from the back of the room. The students were slow to join him, but Dr. Burnstein quickly followed his lead.

"Deuteronomy Jackson," Tony said. "Come talk for a few minutes to the class. Please."

"You want me to come down there and talk about how you steal money to get rich?" Deuteronomy said from the back of the room.

The class cheered and burst into applause.

"In a manner of speaking, yes," Tony said.

Deuteronomy strode to the front of the auditorium. As he walked onto the stage area, Tony said, "I don't know how much you heard of what I was talking about."

"I heard it," Deuteronomy said.

"Well, my premise is you don't get to be extremely wealthy by just taking what the market will give you. By making a fair return on investment. Does that sound right to you?"

Deuteronomy scowled.

"I should point out that I'm pretty sure my friend Mr. Jackson is by far the wealthiest man in this room," Tony said. "Forgive me, Deuteronomy."

"Now wait a goddamn minute," Deuteronomy said, reaching for the microphone. He took it from Tony and spoke into it. "You trying to get a black man to come down here and say he's a goddamned thief?"

The class laughed. Nervously.

"I mean," Deuteronomy said, "Hath not a nigger eyes?"

There was more nervous laughter in the auditorium. Dr. Burnstein was visibly ill at ease. He laughed the loudest.

"Tell them, then," Tony said. "They all want to know how to get really, stinking rich. Tell em how you do it."

"Well," Deuteronomy said, "You learn to maximize your return on investment."

The laughter was louder.

"What can I say?" Deuteronomy said, "You don't get rich running a goddamned charity."

The auditorium burst into applause.

Tony bowed toward Deuteronomy.

"No," Deuteronomy said to the class, "you want to get rich? You got to be the meanest nigger in the bunch."

This was greeted with a shocked silence.

"People got to know," he continued, "that when the money flows, it ain't flowing to them. It's flowing to your ass."

There was more silence.

"And they got to know," he said, "if it don't flow to your ass-you gonna grab em by they balls."

He reached down and grabbed Tony Jones by the crotch so hard Tony shouted out. Right there in front of God and the University of North Carolina at Chapel Hill. Deuteronomy squeezed, and Tony struggled to get away.

"Ain't that right, my brother?" Deuteronomy said. He handed Tony the microphone, patted him on the back, and walked off the stage.

Dr. Ralph Burnstein was ashen white.

The Chancellor stood motionless at the back door to the auditorium.

"Well, you wanted to see how it really works," Tony Jones said to them all. He grinned with delight.

The class rose to its feet in ovation.

48

Portia rarely visited her father's house in Edgartown, Massachusetts. The stately, Cape-Cod-style mansion overlooked Katama Bay. Its dozen bedrooms could house quite a party, and they often had while Portia's parents were alive.

It's not that Portia didn't like Martha's Vineyard. She had the fondest memories of her childhood summers there with her parents.

She just found the house too large, the island too changed with development and too crowded. And the place on the whole reminded her of how alone she felt.

When Bass proposed a house party that fall, she didn't resist. They could fill several of the guest rooms. The weather would be perfect. She could have her father's Herreshoff sloop rigged and tied up at the dock for the first time in so many years. She could take her fiancé sailing in Nantucket Sound and show him the places her father used to take her on Chappaquiddick.

The more she thought about it, the more she felt her love for Bass grow. She had two days off from school the first week in October- fall break. Bass arranged to fly the party up in Tony's jet.

Caretakers kept Portia's place ready for visits on a moment's notice, all expenses funded by the estate trust. Portia occasionally let her parents' friends or more distant relatives use the place, free of charge, so it would be maintained and kept open.

She and Bass would go on this trip, and yes, Nerissa and Gray, now an item, and Jessica and Lorenzo, and Tony and a date. Portia had wondered who the date might be- but the morning they were to leave, Tony called to cancel. He was facing a terrible business crisis, Bass told her. She felt so sorry for Tony. Should they stay home and lend him moral support? she asked. Bass said there was no need, he was sure.

Portia was happy. She hadn't been this anxious to go to Edgartown since her father died.

The weather was unseasonably balmy the first week of October. She could tell as they deplaned that she may indeed get to take her love for a sail on the Sound.

When the limousine dropped them at the front door, Portia quickly showed the others to their rooms. The moment she had a chance to herself, she ran like a girl into the back garden and down the long slope to the boathouse.

There the Herreshoff bobbed in a brisk easterly at the dock. It was freshly painted and varnished, and the mainsail was furled neatly on the spruce boom.

Portia sat down on the dock, her feet dangling over the sloop. The breeze blew her hair onto her cheeks, and she was deeply, deeply filled with joy.

She had been there a long time. Longer than her duties as hostess really would allow. Bass found her there. He sat and put his arm around her. She told him about the sloop, how she had sailed it with her father so many times to the beaches on the Sound side of Chappaquiddick.

Dinner was catered by a restaurant in Edgartown, a new place Portia had never heard of. The caretaker agency had recommended it. She had dinner served on the porch overlooking the harbor. The windows were drawn shut to keep out the cool, evening breeze. Moonlight was lovely on the bay below.

They all drank too much wine.

Bass rose to give a toast to the most beautiful woman he had ever known. Beautiful in ways he had never known. He said he never thought he would marry a second-grade teacher. A public school teacher. A woman with a home in Edgartown she never used.

A woman who was so... he stumbled for words. Bass was not one for words.

A woman who was so together, he said.

"How the hell did I get so lucky?" he said.

"And I find out she can sail, too."

Gray rose from his seat and lifted his glass. "I'd like to propose a toast, too."

"We haven't finished Bass's toast yet," Jessica said.

"The great mouth must speak," Bass said. "Go ahead."

"No seriously," Gray said. "And don't call me the great mouth. You know I don't like it. I don't talk more than anyone else.

Everyone roundly laughed.

"I was rising to toast not just our beautiful hostess, but her equally beautiful friend, Nerissa," Gray said, "who is just as fascinating, just as humble, just as charming, and just about as oblivious to whether anyone has any money or not. Which is a very good thing in my case. I'm rising to toast to both women, who both deserve it, not that other beautiful women at this table don't, also."

"Here, here," Bass said.

But Gray didn't sit down. "I have something serious I'd like to say. Seriously."

They laughed.

"No seriously. This is a solemn occasion. What I'd like to say," and he pulled a ring box out of his pocket and fell to one knee beside Nerissa, "is would you marry me, Nerissa?"

There was silence. A kind of shocked silence.

49

Forth from the silence came the blaring ring of a cell phone.

And so we come more or less to the end of Act III, Scene ii of The Merchant of Venice. *Two pairs of lovers are nearly betrothed. Marriage is inevitable. We can have no couriers. None that I can imagine, that is, so I've had the telephone ring with news of Tony's troubles.*

Tony's character would, of course, be Antonio in the play (if you're familiar with the play, or if you remember it from school years.) In fact, Tony's real name is Antonio Ricardo Bass, Jr. But that's neither here nor there. I have to have a telephone ring, I think. You can't really have a courier arrive with this vital plot development in the 21st century.

I'm trying to imagine what the cell phone looks like in 2008. In the fall. Right after the collapse of Lehman Brothers triggered what Alan Greenspan called "the worst financial crisis in human history."

What did my cell phone look like back then? It was a Palm Treo 650, I believe. Rather clunky. Nothing like you would have today. It could access the Internet, I remember, but I certainly wouldn't think of it as a Smart Phone. It was an expensive thing, something I used in my business. As I remember, it was beginning to get a bit out of date by that time, because the financial trouble had been coming on for a couple of years, and I was trying not to spend as much.

Oh well, you won't be particularly interested in the details of how I imagine this story. You're only really interested in following along in the story, aren't you? You're beginning to be irritated by these interruptions, unless...

Unless you somehow have become interested in me. In my story.

Who the hell is this guy? you may be asking yourself. Why does he keep breaking in?

You may or may not have known the story you were reading was a pastiche of The Merchant of Venice. *If you ever read that play in school, so long ago, you might now begin to see how our plot was stolen from it. But what does it really matter? You may say.*

Why, I wonder, do I have these people in Edgartown? October is really a bit chilly for an expedition to Edgartown, I imagine. It has to do with my sailing trips there. It was such a wonderful place. So prosperous. So over-the-top with wealth, but in a more tasteful way, perhaps.

There were some mega-yachts, yes. But in my mind's eye, as I remember our forty-foot sloop lying on a mooring in Katama Bay, looking up at the houses on the hill where I imagine Portia and her dear ones gathered, I remember a harbor full of boats belonging to the merely affluent. I remember the town and its streets packed in early July with members of the one-percent. Sure, there would have been some of the very wealthy, I presume, walking in those hordes of nattily-dressed vacationers, but most of them looked like us.

How did I get there?

How did I get back there?

Why am I rewriting a Shakespeare play, setting it in the year leading up to the Great Recession?

That is, perhaps, a more interesting story than the one I've been telling you.

But right now, Deuteronomy Jackson has Tony Jones in his clutches, and he's threatening to cut his balls off.

And as you saw at the beginning of this tale, it looks like he really might do it.

What about Chaqueena in that flimsy, wife-beater t-shirt? Grabbing Tony by the genitals and dragging his butt across the seat of that chair?

She's not in The Merchant of Venice, *is she? Now you may be trying to remember the play. Trying to remember the characters. Or maybe you've never read that play, and it's stinking Shakespeare, for God's sake, and here you were reading a good story, and you're starting to get pissed off.*

Part 2

1

Well, they had Tony Jones bound and gagged and naked. They had him duct taped to a straight-backed chair, in the mobile home near the makeshift shooting range where Lancelot had taken Bass to shoot the Uzi.

Actually, at this point, Deuteronomy and Chaqueena had not shown up at the mobile home. There were just a couple of Deuteronomy's thugs there- the two who dragged Tony out of his car when he pulled up to his Myers Park home that evening.

The thugs threw him in the back of a panel van and punched him in the face many, many times, so now his eyes were swollen nearly shut. Dried blood clung to his upper lip and the corners of his mouth and chin.

His mouth was duct-taped shut, with a rubber ball in it.

The henchmen communicated with Chaqueena via cell phone that their orders had been completed.

Tony wasn't sure who these two were. He was confident they were working for Deuteronomy.

The phone that was ringing up in Edgartown was Bass's phone. The laughter when the phone call interrupted Gray's proposal was still going on.

Gray stayed down on his knee, anxiously studying Nerissa's expression.

Bass glanced at the screen of his telephone and rejected the call.

"Oh darling, yes," Nerissa said. "Yes, darling, I'll marry you."

She led Gray up from his knee, and they embraced.

Bass's phone rang again. He glanced irritatedly at the screen, saw it was the same number, and once again rejected the call.

2

So who the hell am I, and why am I inventing this novel based on a Shakespeare play?

I have a lot of time on my hands. Basically- I lost my balls in the Great Recession.

Which had quite an impact on me.

For the past several semesters, when it was time to show my English 102 classes a Shakespeare play- I've shown Al Pacino's movie version of The Merchant of Venice.

Let's face it- I was seriously bored.

There. I'm watching this movie over and over. Don't get me wrong- it's a pretty good movie. The play itself is damn good, but it is a Shakespeare play, for goodness' sake, and this is stinking English 102. So as I watch the movie, over and over, semester after semester, I start imagining this parallel story, in the parallel universe of the Twenty-First Century. I imagine myself as a writer who can tell a story as well as Shakespeare does. I can grab my audience like Al Pacino when he takes that huge knife and goes to cut the pound of flesh out of Jeremy Irons' breast. It's a big, long knife with a rounded blade, like those knives Arab terrorists use to saw off hostages' heads on the Internet.

My students always gasp at this point. And listen, these are community-college freshmen. They don't get anything. But they gasp with horror as Pacino makes his move.

"Tarry a little!" Portia says firmly, right before the knife begins to cut.

And there begins the best part of the story.

3

I wonder if the poor little loan officer who grabbed me by the balls that day gave a shit about me. Because he was one scheming, double-crossing, duplicitous little bastard.

Well, the truth is, when he stood up to shake my hand, he had tears in his eyes. He really did. I had just had my balls yanked out of my scrotum, and there I was giving the bastard a man-hug. I really did. Why in the world did I do that? Why would I care?

It's sort of like asking why Tony Jones would care about Deuteronomy Jackson. But he does. In this story I stole from Shakespeare and then made up, Tony has this love-hate thing going on with Deuteronomy. (Hey, don't just blame me. You were going along with this.)

But is Tony really me? And how in the hell could that sleek, evil genius Deuteronomy even compare to the red-faced banker who ruined my life? I'm asking myself those questions.

You're probably still wishing I would shut up about myself and get on with your story.

4

"This is really strange," Bass said after he had listened to the message on his cell phone.

"What is strange?" Portia asked him.

"Everything. What the hell?"

Bass stood and walked away from the table.

"Darling," Portia said. She started after him.

"Give me a minute, will you?" Bass said. Portia watched him go. She could see him in the entry hall. She saw him open the door and call for Lancelot.

She saw the black man meet him in the doorway, and she saw Bass close the door to block her sight.

5

When it all came down around my ears, I had no instinct at all to keep it from others.

At least in my eyes, I had nothing to hide. Anyone could know I was going broke. Anyone who cared to listen would hear my tale of injustice and woe. How it really wasn't my fault. How the world fell apart around us all, and everybody began to act in the craziest and most unpredictable...

But enough.

Bass's instinct was just the opposite. He immediately felt the need to obfuscate. Would Tony want Portia to know the money was borrowed, he asked himself? Should anyone know the money was borrowed from the biggest drug dealer in Charlotte? Bass was frozen. He didn't know how to handle this.

"Holy shit!" Lancelot said, when Bass told him of the phone message. "He's going cut Tony's balls off."

Lancelot began pacing.

"I mean that bastard gonna kill your brother. That ain't right," Lancelot said, amazed. "Tony Jones is the man. He gonna kill the motherfucking man. That motherfucker going crazy."

"He can't kill Tony Jones," Bass said. "I mean you don't just pick up Tony Jones and kill him."

"The motherfucker crazy," Lancelot said.

What Bass and Lancelot didn't know at this point was that the Lehman Brothers collapse had erased the value of the bonds Deuteronomy Jackson's daughter had sold him. So Deuteronomy wasn't so much crazy as he was mad as hell. Or he was heartbroken. Or he was stressed out. Way beyond stressed out. *The way I was when I learned that everything was gone, that I was going under.*

It makes you do some very crazy things.

6

My plan had been to liquidate anything we could get our hands on. I told my wife we could pull the kids out of college and leave on a sailing trip around the world.

Don't laugh. I was serious. At least I thought I was.

My wife threatened divorce. My attorney brought me around to reality. I was trapped.

That just made me madder. I started going crazy. It didn't seem so crazy at the time, but as I think about what eventually happened...

Listen, let's talk about sex for a bit. We all think about it. All the time. Especially at work, right? When we're supposed to be working, and we're with people that we really have no business having sex with- we think about it constantly. You know, if we thought about sex as often when we were home in bed with our spouses, we'd get in a lot less trouble.

But we don't. We're human. We think about sex to entertain ourselves. We create these nasty daydreams to get ourselves through the boring sales call or the boring staff meeting or the vapid futility of our seeming fate.

Do you think college professors are any different?

So there I was, former CFO of the largest development firm in the Southeastern U.S. Now I'm out of work, and frigging broke, and I take this job at an historically black college teaching Accounting as an adjunct professor.

In case you don't know, "adjunct" means you work part-time, you have no tenure, you have no benefits, and you get paid shit. I mean shit. We're talking less than twenty grand a year, and sometimes a lot less, even if you teach a full load of classes.

Of course, the colleges charge full tuition for the classes you teach, and the poor students don't really know (or care) whether you're an adjunct professor or a full-time professor.

Oh, the colleges make a killing at it. Nowadays something like sixty-five percent of the instructors at America's universities and colleges are adjuncts.

It's a crime. But it's the kind of crime that goes on all across our country these days. You know it. No matter what you do for a living, you see this sort of crime in all directions. A few folks at the top make all the big bucks. Everybody else gets squeezed down to nothing. We've all been living it for a while, now. For years. Or is it for decades?

So here am I, former CFO, formerly a happy member of the one percent, firm in my conviction that I had arrived in that comfy spot through my own perspicacity, hard work, and boundless merit, and now I was broke- and I mean BROKE. I was a part-time accounting professor at what my former mentor and CEO regularly referred to, in my presence, as "that nigger college."

I'd walk to the front of an auditorium in the business school, stroll up to the podium and set my briefcase on it. There I was, lily-white, still dressed like I wasn't the failure I really was. These kids were hanging on my every word when I started to lecture them on Accounting 101. I was the MAN. I was the MAN standing right in front of them.

*The syllabus opened with a photo- me on my fifty-foot sail-
boat in the Bahamas. Of course, now it was the bank's fifty-
foot sailboat, and I'd never own anything like it again. But I
didn't tell them that. I was pretending to be the MAN, and they
were buying that lie like it was Powerball tickets.*

*At least I thought that was what they were thinking. Now
that some time has gone by, I suspect a great many of them
were just thinking about sex.*

7

You're wondering, "What the hell is going on here? This bastard interrupts MY story that I'm reading and enjoying. First he tells me he's an English instructor at a community college, and now he tells me he's a former CFO and an adjunct accounting professor at a- well, an historically black college, COME ON!"

Do you think I'm lying to you? Have you not doubted my veracity from the beginning? When you picked this book from the other novels available for your fantasy reading, were you not looking for the most reliable liar you could find as an author?

Of course. You were looking for the best story.

Now, in this particular case, you have not caught me in a lie. I hold both a Master's Degree in English Literature and a Masters in Business Administration.

So, when I was flat broke and out of work, I was paradoxically qualified to teach at the college level in two completely unrelated fields.

Which may be why I found The Merchant of Venice *so appealing. You see, Shakespeare's grasp of business is just so spot-on. It's brilliant.*

Was that because Shakespeare was such a brilliant busi-nessman himself? We know very little about Shakespeare, but we do know he was a genius of the very highest order, almost a divine genius. A conduit, if you will, of the word of... of what-ever the hell it is. I don't know what to call it, or how a human mind could conceive of it, or exactly what we understand when we hear it, or why I love it so much. But nobody knows what to call it or how to put it into words. We just somehow recognize...

Back to the story. Sorry.

So I was up there in the front of that auditorium at that his-torically black university, facing that crowd of rowdy, slack-faced students, thinking I had fallen so far. So very, very far. Wondering how it could have happened to me. How it could have happened so fast? Why had my whole life, my whole world- my whole country- fallen apart in the space of a few years? And I was thinking how I really needed poetry in my life, poetry of the highest and very most profound sort. I didn't give a frank shit about management accounting any more...

And then she walked in. Late. Down the center aisle of the auditorium.

8

Could all my descriptions of Chaqueena begin to paint her? That's who she was, really. I can't lie. That's exactly who she was. Everything about her. Even though she never did any of those things (or almost none of them). Chaqueena is her. There is no doubt in my mind. I suppose there should be no doubt about it in your mind, now.

She was wearing brown overalls. The pants legs were short, and underneath was a tight t-shirt, so her breasts swayed to and fro as she walked down the stairs. She never took her eyes off me as she walked.

"Hello," I said. I stepped to the front of the auditorium and held out my hand.

There was a silence in the classroom.

"Hello to you," she said.

She just stared at my outstretched hand.

She took a seat three rows up, right on the aisle, and crossed those impossible legs into the aisle.

The class laughed at me.

I blushed, I'm sure. I stumbled back to the podium and mumbled my way through a roll call. It took a while, with some hundred students in the class. We were supposed to do it carefully the first day, because the school didn't get its tuition money from the government if the financial aid recipients didn't actually show up for class.

Charmeka _____. That was her. She raised her hand and said she was there, and I stopped, breathless, actually.

"You can call me Meka," she said. She really didn't do any-thing to encourage me in my idiocy, but I was done for.

All those undergrads. All that daydreaming about sex. All of us. All the time. Every class. But here was a daydream that was going to wreck my life.

9

I'd better get back to Tony Jones before you give up on me.

Tony was duct-taped to a straight-backed chair far out in Central North Carolina.

And Tony knew what he had gotten himself into. He knew how he had gotten himself into it. In some way, he knew, he had willed himself into this very situation.

Why had he done it? He wondered.

He watched the thugs guarding him. They smelled of cologne and marijuana smoke. Their eyes were vapid.

They sat idly, awaiting their orders, as if idleness were the state to which they had born, as if it were their manifest destiny in life, to be punctuated only with sporadic bouts of intoxication, sex, and violence. Nothing else could come forth from these creatures, he imagined.

Their lips bulged ignorantly. They stared forth into space.

"I ain't tole that mufucker shit he be fuckin wi me I cock he ass. Mufuckin skanky ass ho all up in he shit."

"Sheeyut."

"Big titty. BIG titty. Stick dem big titty my face. I fuck dat bitch up."

"Heh, heh, heh," the laugh was...

Subhuman.

MARSHALL EVANS

That was the word that came to Tony's mind. He couldn't help it. He immediately felt a little bad about it.

Subhuman. Yes, in fact, he told himself, these were subhuman creatures. And goddamnit if he was going to feel bad about making that judgment. Now that they were plotting his horrific mutilation and death. Why the hell not admit he hated them for what they were? He despised them. They were, indeed, subhuman. They didn't have to be that way. They chose to be that way. Utterly uneducated. Utterly uncultured. Utterly disconnected from the kinds of people Tony had moved among all his life.

One of the thugs smiled. He displayed a ridiculous mouth full of gold-capped teeth.

"How much that grill cost you?" his fellow inquired.

Jesus, thought Tony.

The other thug stroked his fingertip across his mouth.

"Hey, you gotta ask..." he said, his teeth glittering.

His fellow stared blankly- baffled.

"You gotta ask, mufuckah, you caint fode it," the thug continued. He laughed uproariously.

His fellow was unamused. He sulked.

"You mufuckin wish, mufuckuh," the golden-mouthed one gloated.

"All that glitters is not gold," his fellow said.

"Sheeyut."

A stony silence ensued.

Tony wanted to vomit.

"Fuck you, mufuckah."

"Yeh? Well, we see."

The golden-mouthed one glared at Tony.

"What you lookin at muthafuckah?"

Tony glared back at him.

"The big man," the golden-mouthed thug said. "The big white rich muthafuckah. I ain't scared of you."

He was lying, Tony knew. Tony knew lies.

"Muthafuckah stare at me, I fuck you up."

Tony stared at him.

The thug jumped from his seat and brandished a pistol. He cocked the pistol to chamber a live round. He aimed the gun at Tony's head.

"Muthafuckah! I fuck you up."

Tony stared at him. Tony made no move. He made no effort to speak through the duct tape on his mouth.

The thug raised the pistol like he was going to hit Tony in the face with it.

"You muthafuckah. I fuck yo white ass up."

Subhuman, Tony thought. Subhuman. Tony slightly shook his head in disgust.

"Shake yo fuckin head, muthafuckah!" The thug was screaming. He lowered the pistol and pointed it at Tony's head.

Tony stared at him.

The gun fired. Tony felt the powder blast on his face. He felt the fiery bullet pass him.

The thug fired. Again and again, barely missing. On purpose.

The trailer was a chaos of noise and broken glass.

The thug fired again and again, rapid fire, until the magazine was empty.

Tony had pissed himself. His urine ran off the chair and onto the floor.

The thug stuck his face next to Tony's and screamed, "Muthafuckah! I fuck you up!"

Subhuman, Tony thought. Not a human being.

The other thug laughed. "Deuteronomy Jackson goan fuck you up, muthafuckah. You better get you shit together."

The golden-mouthed thug screamed inarticulately and threw his pistol. It crashed through a broken window and sailed out of the trailer.

Stupid-as-hell subhuman, thought Tony.

This was getting to be more fun than he ever imagined. When was his friend Deuteronomy going to make his appearance? Tony hoped Chaqueena would come with Deuteronomy. He hoped she would be looking hot. Smoking hot. He lost himself in the idea of Chaqueena walking naked in pink, wet sand.

The way she moved her hips when her feet sank in.

10

In The Merchant of Venice, *when Bassanio discovers Antonio has gone broke, and Shylock threatens to collect the pound of flesh Antonio now owes him, Bassanio quickly confesses his problem to fair Portia.*

Oh, I'm sorry. You may not even know what I'm talking about here. This is the plot of Shakespeare's play. And if you don't know it, who cares? Trust me. We've been following the plot exactly up to this point in our story.

There is a tightly tangled knot here, if you think about it. But Shakespeare untangles it adroitly- with nothing more than Portia's natural grace.

Shakespeare unties the knot in a few lines. Bassanio confesses. Portia forgives.

Bassanio owes a debt of love to his friend, she says, and he must go pay it. As for the debt of money, a staggering amount of money in Renaissance Venice- well, who gives a damn? She doesn't. The audience doesn't. Shylock does, but we hate him for it.

Yeh, o.k. You don't care. Then- in the story I'm making up for you, on that beautiful bluff in Martha's Vineyard, on a brilliant October evening, when stars filled the chilled sky and moonlight danced in countless shimmerings laid across the sea

157

by the southeast breeze, our fair Portia would be no less gracious, would she? Bass would confess with no less dispatch. Portia's grace would almost precede the confession. Her prescription of love and fealty to Tony would flow just as naturally.

I would handle this knotted bit of plot just as.... Well, we can only imagine. We can only dream and hope. That is really all we are, isn't it? Just dreams and hopes and love. That is all we ever can be. We are such stuff as dreams... The part of me that dreams higher than a man can reasonably dream is, perhaps, the part of me that is worthwhile. So let me dream.

11

Let us dream together, you and I, as their evening lies stretched out against the sky like a lover fantasized within a fable. Let us go, through half-forgotten streets, that summering retreat where restless nights are spent in chic, boutique hotels, midst sawdust restaurants with oyster shells- streets that follow like a timeless argument of invidious intent to lead you to the overwhelming question.

Oh, do not ask, "What is it?"

Let us go and make our visit.

"There are some shrewd contents in that call he took," said Portia to Nerissa, "that steal the color from my lover's face. Some dear one dead- Or nothing in the world could turn so much the disposition of that dear, kind man."

Portia rose and followed Bass, emerging where the whispering breeze stirred golden alden leaves in the floodlight. She found him huddled with his body man.

"Bass," she said, "I am half of you, and you must freely share the half of anything that phone call brought."

And so he told her everything.

"It's only that? Twelve million? Let's go tomorrow morning to be married. I'll wire him twenty-million by end of day.

"Tomorrow morning," she said. "We'll be married at County Courthouse in Edgartown. I'll call my friend the judge this evening. We'll pay this debt, make Jackson happy, and all will be settled."

12

Ah, fair Portia. What a creature of the imagination! Surely this woman could not really exist. The beauty, the love, the infinite power to forgive, the modesty, the unimaginable wealth, for which she seems to care nothing.

Which Portia am I talking about? Ours *or Shakespeare's?*

Why both, of course. Do you know anyone like that? (Shakespeare's Portia is one of his most magnificent heroines. Famously so.)

Of course not. You never have known any real person like Portia. Or Portia. But you love imagining her. What is it about that character that makes her so delicious to imagine?

The key role of Portia in this story is.... Well, that's kind of complicated. I was about to say her key role was as Bassanio's love interest up to this point (Well, or as Bass's love interest.) But she really seems to have had some other role. She's complex, isn't she?

The suitors who failed. Remember them?

The relationship with the father. Remember that?

The anguish over her failures to marry. The anguish over the burden of her wealth. The anguish over that kind of secret she shares with her best friend. The thing they seem to know, but we don't.

She's more complex than I had thought.

Now we're working our way into the part of the story where Portia becomes the central character. Her intellect and daring, not to mention her cross-dressing skills, must save Antonio from the clever, vengeful, and impossibly complex Shylock.

(Shylock, is of course, Deuteronomy Jackson *in our newly copied story.) You've heard of Shylock, I'll bet, even if you're not familiar with Shakespeare's play. But try not to let Shylock distract you. Let's try to wrench ourselves back to the real story...*

Our Portia must save Tony from that Deuteronomy Jackson.

Because what you really want- just as Shakespeare's audience wanted- is for the clear villain to be defeated by truth and beauty, Christian charity and intelligence.

That's what will make you happy, right?

What if, instead, I just let Deuteronomy Jackson take that bread knife, grab Tony Jones by his genitals, and just saw them them off, as the blood gushes and Tony screams into the rubber ball taped in his mouth.

And what if Chaqueena watches?

You aren't going to want that, are you?

You're not going to be happy if that happens.

But what would happen in real life, if you weren't imagining this whole story? If I weren't dreaming it up for your entertainment?

What if it was real fucking life? Huh?

13

I began fantasizing about Chaqueena immediately.

O.k. Her name really was Chaqueena. It wasn't Charmeka as I told you.

God, if I had to admit to you all the fantasies I had.

I screwed her on the table in the adjunct instructors' lounge. I locked the door, turned off the lights, and held her golden-brown legs up in the air as I thrust...

Well, that was before I got to the end of the hallway after that first class. I was following behind her, not fifteen feet behind. She knew it. She could feel my eyes on her. She was working it.

I often lusted after my young students. Hell, I often lusted after my middle-aged students. I was a normal person. I was bored with my job. I was thinking about sex all the time.

She was electric.

I was just marveling at the body, at the walk, at the clothes, at the attitude... when she spun around in the middle of the hallway and faced me.

I stopped and stared like an imbecile.

"Mr. Marshall," she said. "That's your name, ain't it? Mr. Marshall?"

She took a few steps and stood right in front of me. She had a sexual presence I had never seen before. I caught my breath.

"You act like you ain't really a teacher," she said. "Like you been something else all your life."

I laughed.

"You ain't no college professor," she said, grinning. "I can tell. This ain't you."

And before I could answer- before I could regain my composure and take control of the conversation- she smiled the most endearing smile. She turned and walked away, into the crowd of students at class change.

14

My Portia, alas, was no Portia.

My Portia had been married to me for twenty-five years already. She plucked gray hairs from her head every morning at a vanity in our bedroom.

She was no billionaire. I can recall few times when she had been gracious about money.

When I went broke, she displayed little in the way of backbone. She displayed little in the way of grace. She raged. She sulked. She fled to her girlfriend's home in Florida for a week. She screamed in our attorney's office as we talked about losing our home and pulling the children out of college.

But she stayed. She stayed and worked through it. She stayed, as you will see, far past the point where anyone would have expected her to leave.

I wish I could say she was fair Portia, endowed with beauty and wealth. Surrounded by suitors from around the globe.

But she was my wife. She had been for a very long time.

And I was going to treat her very, very badly before it was all over.

15

Our fictional Portia, on the other hand, arranged to marry Bass the following morning. On less than twelve hours' notice, she shone forth at the Dukes County Courthouse, wearing a beige dress as beautiful and graceful as any bridal gown you ever imagined.

Imagine her now, if you will. The New England courthouse. The autumn leaves floating to the ground. The sidewalks and street and small lawns covered with golden fall.

The radiance of her smile. The devotion of her new husband- battling with his distraction and concern for his brother.

She put Bass in a taxi right outside the courthouse, right after the ceremony, and sent him on his way to the airport. Her father's private jet (previously maintained by the estate trust- but now Portia's) would take Bass and his friends to North Carolina by lunch time.

You may wonder why they didn't simply call the police. This was clearly a kidnapping. It was extortion under the threat of murder.

Well, let me explain that part.

16

You see, after the ill-fated Bahamas trip, Bass had the captain of Deuteronomy's yacht take the entire party back to Miami.

Bass might want you to believe he didn't know what cargo he was carrying for Deuteronomy. But Deuteronomy had found a way to let him know.

Deuteronomy told Bass's brother.

The night before they left, Deuteronomy pulled Tony aside for a walk in the forest of his Exumas island escape. They came to the open area overlooking the other islands. Wind waves lapped at the rocks beneath them. There was Deuteronomy's favorite bench. He asked Tony to sit with him.

"Tony," he said. Moonlight illuminated the myriad small cays rising from the water in front of them. A gentle trade wind blew.

"I like you Tony," he said. "I can't say I'm crazy about this crowd of clowns you travel with, but I like a fucker with balls."

"I'm glad you think I've got balls, Deuteronomy," Tony said.

"Well, you got balls enough to ask me for twelve million dollars. Nobody comes to me with anything like that."

"What's your point, Deuteronomy?" Tony said. "I see an opportunity, I go for it. You got to raise money to pursue business opportunities. Part of it. You know that."

"I do. I do," said Deuteronomy.

They stared at the Exumas in the moonlight.

"Tony," Deuteronomy said, "I'm going to get you to do some bidness for me."

"What business would that be, exactly?" Tony said.

"Well, ain't none of your bidness to know," Deuteronomy said. "And, if you want to know the truth of it, I ain't asking. I'm telling you."

"We've got our deal," Tony said. "You aren't going to start crab walking on our deal."

"Oh hell no," Deuteronomy said. "Like you say, we got our deal. I do a deal, I stick with it. I follow through to the letter. Cause let me tell you, Tony. In my bidness, you start fucking around with people, and you don't just end up being talked about at the Apex Club. You end up being dead."

There was silence.

"No, Tony," Deuteronomy said. "Let me tell you what's going down. When you and your friends go back to Miami tomorrow in that boat you chartered, you gonna be carrying some cargo for me."

"Wait a damn minute," Tony said.

"No." Deuteronomy said. "You wait a damn minute."

Tony stood up. "Fuck no," he said. "I'm not getting involved in any drug running. Do you have any idea who you're dealing with here?"

"Yeh," Deuteronomy said. "I'm dealing with a man who already laundered thirty-three million dollars in cash for me."

"What the hell are you talking about?"

"Twelve million for your brother's loan," Deuteronomy said, "and twenty-one million for the boat. And by the way, thank you very much."

"I didn't launder any goddamn money."

"You may be too fucking stupid to know you did it," Deuteronomy said, "but I can assure you you did. The FBI and the Treasury Department would be delighted to confirm what I'm telling you. Why don't you call them up and ask?

"They can pretty much see money laundering when they look right at it," Deuteronomy continued. "The trouble is, they ain't as good as a smart street nigger. And the best bankers in Charlotte."

"What are you talking about" Tony said. He was furious.

"Tony," said Deuteronomy, "you need to calm down. Somebody gonna hear you throwing a tantrum. You liable to have all kinds of loose lips knowing your fucking bidness."

Tony thought for a moment. He sat back down on the bench.

"All I'm saying," Deuteronomy said, "is you gonna do a little more bidness- just as easy as the first bidness you did for me. You didn't even know you was doing that."

"Jesus," Tony said.

"My aunt Irma wouldn't like you taking the Lord's name in vain," Deuteronomy said.

"Jesus fucking Christ," Tony said.

"He ain't got nothing to do with it," Deuteronomy said.

There was a silence.

"And listen," Deuteronomy said. "It ain't all bad news. I'm gonna pay you for doing this little bit of bidness. And you ain't against making money, is you? Last I heard that's what Tony Jones is all about. Making that stroke."

Tony just shook his head in the darkness.

"Ain't you?" Deuteronomy said. And he put his arm around Tony's shoulder and hugged him to him. "Tony Jones got the biggest balls any fucker I ever met."

17

This maps so well to my story. Boy, if anybody really knew my whole story. It would be obvious to them that I'm following it just as closely as I'm following The Merchant of Venice.

Let's be realistic here. When you read something, you match it up with the reality of your own life, don't you? You have to imagine the story, and the only way you can really do that is to map it out over the landscape of your own life- your own emotions and experiences. If you didn't have that as a base for your imagination, you couldn't just read words on a page and turn them into a comprehensible story.

So, let's say you are in freshman English class, and that professor or graduate student you hated so much is making you read a Shakespeare play, The bloody Merchant of fucking Venice, *for Christ's sake.*

And you read it, this time, instead of just reading Spark notes.

Or maybe you actually go on Youtube and watch the movie- with Al Pacino as Shylock, and Jeremy Irons as Antonio- and let's say you actually start to get into it.

And let's take a leap of imagination. Perhaps a leap too far, in your case, but let's say that Pacino and that damnable English professor actually get you over the hump. You start to see the story is not just good, it's sublime beyond words, a human achievement beyond imagining.

You've got to have something inside you that matches up with what Shakespeare put out there. It's got to match up with what's in your heart, right?

And how did what's in your heart get in there?

Did your experience with your reality put it in there?

Or maybe it was in there already.

Could that be the case?

18

Outwardly- outside of my imagination at least- my rela-tionship with Chaqueena was more or less appropriate that whole semester. The whole time I taught at the historically black college. A year later it got out of hand.

I was teaching Survey of World Literature at the commu-nity college. Chaqueena was attending classes there, now. She had dropped out of her private, black college. She was likely to drop out of the much-less-expensive community college, too, I knew. Fewer than ten percent of our female, African-American students ever graduated from our college.

I made out with Chaqueena before that semester was over. It happened in the library. Back in the stacks. I saw her going into one of the little study rooms in the corner.

"Chaqueena," I whispered.

"Mr. Marshall," she whispered back, mocking me.

She had been by my office a few times already. I loved chat-ting with her. She was tough. She was my chief adversary in class debates.

Chaqueena had no problem with debate. She thrived on it. When the topic had been exhausted in the classroom, she would come and talk in my office. Her favorite topic was the Black Lives Matter movement. She pointed out how the system kept the poor down and lifted the rich up- how it marginalized and oppressed people of color while offering the lighter-skinned a gently sloping path to success.

Chaqueena held that breaking rules was the only way to get ahead, especially for people of color. She could argue passionately and insightfully- with outrageous grammatical lapses- in support of her ideology.

Oh, I loved it. I lusted for her. She seemed, as she demonstrated her intellect and her will, to gather beauty within her. She radiated a kind of femininity I had never really experienced before. It was an electric thing.

She seemed the type that would be swept off her feet only by a thug. By a real criminal. By someone who provided something far outside her own sweep of personality and potential.

I have no idea how it happened.

There I was in the stacks of the library. I had never, ever said anything inappropriate to her. I was a college instructor thirty years her senior. I had imagined many, many inappropriate things about her. I had indulged the most graphic and salacious fantasies- long, breathless fantasies of sex acts my aging body rarely demonstrated any real capability of achieving.

You may find this amusing. You may find it pathetic. In nearly thirty years of marriage, I'd had plenty of fantasies. I'd had plenty of flirtations. I'd had women basically throw themselves at me. But I never acted on it. I was a faithful husband like- well, like you might imagine an adjunct accounting instructor my age might be.

There I was, in the stacks of the library, and Chaqueena beckoned me to come closer.

"Evan," she whispered, "I need to ask you something."

She had never called me Evan before. None of my students called me by my first name.

I followed hastily. She led me into the study room and closed the door behind us. There was a small window in the door. It was a college, for Christ's sake. They had to have windows on the doors. The light was on, and the stacks were fairly dark outside, so anybody who was walking by could see us in that little study room with its desk and four chairs.

"I've got this idea," Chaqueena said. Her voice was quiet and throaty now- no longer whispering. "The paper on Four Quartets. *I was lost at first, but now...."*

"It's a challenging assignment," I said

"I was going to write about how Eliot interweaves themes from the gospels and themes from The Bhagavad Gita," *she said.*

This was not what I expected.

"I mean, I'm not sure how I can put it all into words," she said.

I chuckled, "Well, it's a poem about ineffability," I said.

Chaqueena looked puzzled.

"It's about the ineffability of the ultimate mystery of the universe, isn't it?" I said, smiling like an ass.

"What the fuck does that mean?" she said.

"The mystery...," I began.

"I got that shit," she said. "That word."

"Ineffable?"

"Infuckingeffable"

"You can't say it," I said. "I mean it means you can't put it into words."

"What?"

"Something that is ineffable is incapable of being put into words." I said.

"Well why don't you just say what you mean?" Chaqueena said.

"Well that's the whole point, isn't it?" I said.

"This is just a conspiracy to keep the white man on top," she said. She stood close to me. She was inside my personal space. She had never been there. She could tell she was inside my space. She didn't move.

I couldn't find words to answer her. I couldn't step back.

And then it just happened. I kissed her. Right on the lips. Right on her open mouth.

She kissed me back.

It was like my first kiss when I was a teenager. The warm, velvety tongue. The soft- so-soft lips. She put her arms around me. I put my arms around her, and we kissed.

Her hips, where I had my hands, I can still feel them. So full. So... alive.

Then she pushed herself gently away. She still stood in my personal space. Too close.

"Mr. Marshall," she said. "You can't do that."

"I...," that was all I could say.

"You're married, Mr. Marshall," Chaqueena said.

I was speechless.

"And I'm one of your students."

"I'm sorry," I said. "I'm sorry if this is inappropriate, Chaqueena."

"And besides," she said, laying her hand gently on my cheek. "I'm with somebody."

She kissed me slowly on the lips, plunging her tongue deep into my mouth this time. Then she stopped, and she walked to the other side of the table.

I stood panting like a schoolboy.

"*Mr. Marshall,*" *she said, smiling broadly, "you can't fuck me if you're going to be my professor.*"

19

Why did my wife get the gun? And why is my wife named Portia?

Well, for goodness' sake, her parents gave her that name. Maybe that's one reason I've always liked The Merchant of Venice *so much. Ever since our junior year at Vanderbilt, when I first met her, in the stacks of the library. A chance meeting. A shared accounting class. A homework assignment she found confusing.*

She was so beautiful. She still is, for that matter. Thirty-five years later. How can someone still be so beautiful after all that time? I know I'm blessed. It's just all that other damned stuff. Thirty-five years of it. The beauty doesn't seem to count for as much after all that.

When I was a twenty-year-old fool, I thought Portia was not only beautiful, she was the most together chick I had ever met. She was like the heroine in a Shakespeare comedy. Sort of the ideal woman. In her humanity. Her intelligence. Her beauty. But more than that, in her... what the heck am I trying to say here?

How can you describe Shakespeare's Portia? There is a grace to her. A magnificent grace. What can you say? You can see it. You can understand it. But you can't describe it.

177

My Portia was that way. She was that way for three, four, five years. Even after we graduated and married, I worshiped her. Even when we fought. Even when she was unreasonable. Even when she didn't look good.

But you only have to live with Shakespeare's heroines for two to four hours. A person can be perfect for two to four hours. A whole lot longer than that, and they start to look pretty much like a normal person. That happened, inevitably, to my Portia.

Pregnancy, childbirth, and child rearing played the largest part in it. There are those hormones- the hormones that make a woman a good mother. All good stuff in the long run, I guess, but not a lot of fun to live with.

And there were the hormones in me making me believe I was destined to be so much more than I ever really became.

I became it for a while, but the Great Recession made me who I am today. And that guy...

I fell for Portia. I married her, and I loved her dearly, and I had three daughters with her, and raised them to graduate from college and become self-supporting adults. We went through the long decades of shit together, and we still loved each other.

Then she bought a gun.

We had always been Republicans. Face it, we were white. Our parents were members of the upper-middle class. We were college-educated baby-boomers who belonged to the right fraternity and sorority. We were affluent most of our adult lives. By the time I was CFO of the development company, we were quite affluent. Our cars were nice, as was our condo at the beach, not far from Figure Eight Island. We visited my CEO's house on Figure Eight when we were down there. Our kids

*went to Carolina and State, where they were in the right soror-
ities themselves.*

You've got the picture. We were Republicans, right?

And I'm the one who initially turned the Fox News on.

*I mean looking back on it. You ever notice the chicks on Fox
News? Other than Roger Ailes scheming to get in their pants,
the obvious reason they were all on there was to appeal to the
target demographic. Me.*

*So I brought the propaganda into our home. Portia- dear,
patient, decent Portia- would take her place on the sofa in the
den after dinner, and Bill O'Reilly or Shep Smith would be on,
and, well, we enjoyed the conversation.*

*They talked to us. We'd listen for a while. Then Portia and I
would start talking to each other, and then we'd maybe drift
off to some other entertainment, but, you know, we started to
believe.*

*We were THEIR people. If they couldn't talk to us, who
could they talk to?*

*After a while, the guns got to be part of it. I'd always had
hunting guns- shotguns and rifles. So had Portia's father and
her brothers. It was part of our world.*

*Everybody was doing it. Our friends were talking about it
in supper club. It was just the thing, and then Portia Marshall
asked one day if I would go with her to get a concealed carry
permit, and after a little questioning, I thought, what the hell?
It was something to do together- one of those hobbies we could
pursue as a couple. It would strengthen our marriage.*

*There were classes. There was a little exam. We practiced at
the shooting range.*

*I kind of liked the idea of my Portia with a handgun. Imag-
ine, if you can, Shakespeare's Portia as the beautiful, middle-
aged mother of three college co-eds. And imagine her with her*

legs spread wide on a firing range, that Glock 26 stuck out in both her hands. Imagine that look of fierce determination as she emptied the ten-round magazine into the darkness in front of her.

20

Now imagine, if you could, with that same vividness, with that same glee...

Lancelot stepped out of Portia's jet onto the tarmac at Charlotte Douglas airport. He strode behind Bass and Gray to the waiting limousine. Lancelot unzipped the black carry-on he brought from the plane and pulled out his Uzi machine gun.

"Get in the damn car with that!" Bass called from the limousine. "You'll have the feds all over us."

Lancelot got in the limousine and closed the door. Behind the tinted windows, he fished into his bag and pulled out more guns- a .45-caliber semi-automatic handgun for Bass, a sawed-off shotgun for Gray, and an AK-47 with a folding stock for Lorenzo.

"We ain't fucking with no white pussies here," Lancelot said. "These fuckers will kill your ass."

Lancelot pulled ammunition out of the black bag: Four curved magazines for the Uzi, which he set on the seat beside him. Four loaded magazines for the .45, which he set on the seat beside Gray. A black fanny-pouch full of double-aught buckshot shells for the shotgun. He handed that to Gray. Banana clips for Lorenzo.

"You got thirty rounds in there," Lancelot said. "You can reload fifteen times. But don't none of you try to reload less you hidden out of sight and I tell you it's time to reload. You fuck around with reloading out in the open and these fuckers will blow you away."

"Wait a damn minute," Bass said. "We aren't going in here guns blazing. We're going to talk to these guys."

"You gonna talk Deuteronomy Jackson out of cutting your brother's dick off?" Lancelot said. "Well. I'm interested in hearing exactly what you gonna say to the man."

As the limousine sped out of the private entrance to the airport, Bass sat stupidly, holding an enormous .45 pistol in his hand.

21

Three thousand ducats. That's how much Bassanio needed to fake his way into a marriage with the wealthy Portia. What's a ducat worth? Well, the question really is, what is money worth? That's the point of the whole story, isn't it? Shylock demands one pound of flesh as security on his three-thousand-ducat loan. He makes the argument that a pound of human flesh isn't really worth anything. But of course, the pound of flesh, cut from a living man in Renaissance Europe, would cost the man his life.

A ducat. What is three thousand ducats worth? What's a million dollars worth? What's a billion dollars worth? What's twelve million dollars worth?

Seriously, if I think about it just a little bit, it all sort of starts to vaporize. Can you follow what I'm saying? Is this too fuzzy for you? Is it too unrealistic for you?

Is money just a concept that we tell ourselves is concrete, when in fact it is just about the farthest thing in the world from being concrete?

Money- face it- is nothing but imagination.

One must imagine it into reality. And one must imagine it has worth and power. This requires a massive conspiracy of self-deception. We must all engage with our whole spirits and beings in this delirium. The exercise requires so much of us that we become obsessed with it. We lose ourselves in our hallucination. We wreck our lives over money. We ruin other lives and destroy them in the pursuit of something that is nothing more than pure fantasy.

22

I was such a broken man after my bankruptcy. To my re-vulsion nowadays, I realize the bankruptcy was the most diffi-cult thing I ever experienced- worse than any death I ever lived through- worse by far than any human suffering or disease or real, flesh and blood crisis.

And I damn near killed myself over it.

That Glock 26. They say if you own a gun for personal pro-tection, it's far more likely to kill you or someone you love than it is ever likely to be aimed at a criminal assailant.

I hope you never stare into the barrel end of one of those things.

Imagine that. Well, that's not exactly imaginary. Stick the end in your mouth, and taste the steel and the gun oil and the gunpowder residue.

Imaginary money, nothing but imaginary numbers in some computer memory somewhere, can do something very, very real to you.

There. Calm down.

I never had much paper money until after I went broke, When I was broke, I started cashing my teaching paychecks and keeping the cash in a plastic sandwich bag under my mat-

tress- within reach of the bedside table drawer where Portia kept the Glock.

I imagined the bank or the IRS would draft the money right out of my account if I kept it in a bank. They had the legal right to do so. I knew people who lost their money that way.

The money under the mattress was a bit more real, even though it was nothing but slips of paper with fancy printing.

The money I lost- the big money- the work of a lifetime.- that was nothing but pure imagination. I never saw it. Never touched it. Never smelled it. Never tasted it.

It was never under my bed.

And there I was, with my wife's Glock stuck in my mouth, over the loss of that pure figment of imagination.

I almost did it. I almost wasn't here to make this story up for you.

But, there. That's reality for you. I'm still here.

And you're still reading.

23

I discovered Chaqueena was a stripper.

I heard two male students discussing it after class. I was on my way out of the room. The two students caught me staring at Chaqueena. They laughed and started discussing it in low voices, thinking I couldn't hear.

Oh Jesus, I knew the club. I had been there once, was it eight, ten years earlier? Entertaining clients- sleazy bankers from the Upper Midwest who were in town to discuss mezzanine financing for an apartment complex, I think. Who the hell can remember these things?

I was getting too old to be in a strip club. The strippers were looking too much like my daughters and their friends. Hell, they were younger than my daughters. But I had to entertain the bankers.

And now Chaqueena was a stripper there? The woman for whom I had just risked my marriage and my career?

I know, it's a bit of a stretch to call adjunct teaching a career.

I couldn't get the strip club off my mind. I undressed young Chaqueena in my imagination. She gyrated. Her hips rocked. She beckoned to me. She called me Evan.

When she came to my office next, I could barely contain myself.

"Evan," she said, closing the door behind her. "You don't have to be ashamed. Don't worry about it. I'm not the girl you imagine me to be."

"I," I stammered. "I'm sorry I acted inappropriately. I cannot apologize enough."

"Evan!" she said, with the most amused smile, "I'm the one who kissed you. You the sexiest man I know, you old professor you. Even though I know you ain't really no professor."

With that, she disarmed me, and we spoke as we usually did about the injustices and failures of capitalism in the Twenty-first Century, the exploitation of the weak by the mighty.

I shared with her how I had been brought into the army of the weak and the exploited myself, and how I had come to understand so much, so much more than I had ever imagined might be true.

"You a good man, Mr. Marshall," Chaqueena said. "And you a good teacher, too, you know that? You a lot better professor than you give yourself credit for. I mean you really care about people. Real people. You know what I mean?"

24

So why, in God's name, did I go to that club? Why would I want to see this young woman dancing naked? Yes, she was younger than my daughters. Yes, damnit, I was under no illusions about that.

Why would I want to see her working at a strip club? Why would I possibly want to put myself in that position?

It was four o'clock in the afternoon. I left campus to head home and write. But this time I drove all the way to the far side of Charlotte, out by the airport. Exactly where I remembered. Exactly as I remembered, but with a newer, more elaborate neon sign and an expanded parking lot.

There were about ten customers in the whole place- a dank-smelling room that looked like it could hold a couple of hundred.

Loud, tacky rock music. A lone bartender behind a nearly empty bar.

The cover charge was thirty bucks. I should have turned and walked out. I was going to.

But then I saw her dancing. She was stark naked. Dancing in front of two black guys sitting with their elbows on the runway.

I paid the cover charge with two twenties and forgot to get my change.

A drink. I needed to get a drink first. It would look weird if I went straight up there without getting a drink. I saw the wait-ress with her tray. She was one of the strippers in a string bikini. I stood there at the entrance, trying to decide which way to go, when Chaqueena saw me.

"You!" she shouted, and she pointed straight at me. She stopped dancing momentarily and laughed.

Everybody in the place turned to stare at me.

"I can't believe it's you!" she shouted. She bent over and waggled her breasts at the two men in front of her. She rose, strode rhythmically to the end of the runway nearest me, and grabbed a stripper pole.

She swung her ankles up over her head and inverted herself on the pole, wrapping her legs around it effortlessly.

She beckoned me with her index finger.

"Come on over here and let me dance for you, professor," she said.

25

Chaqueena danced naked for me, in her stiletto heels. Her knees were at my eye level. I stood, I suppose, with my mouth agape, until the waitress came and essentially demanded a drink order from me.

"You like it?" Chaqueena said to me in a somewhat private voice. "It's what you've been daydreaming about, isn't it? And here it was all this time, right here for you to see."

She turned and strutted back down the runway, where the two black guys held up ten-dollar bills to get her attention. On her left thigh she wore a garter belt stuffed with cash. The guys held the bills close to it as she gyrated her Brazilian wax job in front of their faces.

"Come on boys," she said when she'd had enough. "Take care of mama." She took one man's head in her hands and pressed his face against her crotch momentarily as she danced. When she pulled away, he wagged his tongue in the air and stuffed the bill in her garter.

She teased the other man until he tipped her, too.

By then, the song was reaching its climax. She swung her enormous breasts at them, turned and touched her toes in front of them, and the song was over.

"Let's hear it for lovely Chaqueena," an unseen announcer said, and ten or so patrons clapped for her. "Chaqueena."

Chaqueena took the most elegant bow. Like a Broadway headliner. She turned and walked behind the curtain.

The announcer introduced the next act. The abysmal music started again, and another woman emerged on stage.

Chaqueena, now dressed in a string bikini, came from a doorway and walked up to her two primary customers. There was a quick conversation, which I couldn't overhear, and she came straight to my side.

"My professor in the strip club," she said.

"You teach a more interesting class," I said.

"I seem to have your attention," she said. "You gonna make my man jealous. And you don't want to do that."

I saw, then, which of the two black men she was talking about.

They were thugs. Classic thugs. And Chaqueena's thug did not look happy.

"Every black woman needs a good thug nigger," she said to me, smiling.

I didn't know what to say.

"You want to meet Deuteronomy?" she said. "He dying to meet you."

Did Deuteronomy know his open jacket revealed the pistol in his belt? Was he really paying that much attention to me?

26

She introduced him as Deuteronomy Jackson.

"I'm sorry," I said. "I didn't catch that?"

"Deuteronomy," Chaqueena said. "Like the Bible. This Evan Marshall," she said to him. "The professor with the sailboat. Go to the Bahamas all the time."

"I'm sorry," Deuteronomy said, mocking me. "I didn't catch that?"

Chaqueena cut in as I groped for a comeback. "Deuteronomy go to your school," she said. "He taking computer technology."

The real one was a shadow of the one I've imagined for you. So much younger. So much less wealthy, at least when I first met him. But to invent the Shylock of my tale, I only had to take the real young man and project him twenty or so years into the future.

The most remarkable young man I ever met. And I've known a lot of men who became very powerful and very wealthy.

It was his unruffled demeanor. At well over six feet, with a strong body and patrician face, he did the thug thing. He dressed it. He talked it. He acted it with a power that was nothing I'd ever seen. A grace. An almost feminine element to him.

I hated him, of course. My dream student, my dream girl, was completely under the control of this pig of a man. How could she love him?

She obviously did. It was clear I really never had a chance. I knew that before I left the strip club that afternoon. One drink with the real Deuteronomy Jackson, and I was as bewildered as I had ever been in my life.

Chaqueena gave me a big, wet kiss on the cheek when I left. Right there beside Deuteronomy. He didn't care one bit. He knew better.

"Thank you for coming, Evan," she said. "You the best professor a girl ever had."

I stumbled into the afternoon sunshine like a man emerging from a deep dream.

27

I suppose we have to look at how Deuteronomy Jackson, the Real, became Deuteronomy Jackson, the Imagined.

Deuteronomy Jackson, the Real, was a young, horndog thug. Yet I saw my former CEO in his magical, magnetic personality, in the way he saw through all the possibilities and quietly, without tipping his hand, maneuvered himself into advantageous position, entirely willing to stab the other party in the back at the first opportunity.

Our former CEO- the man who made my career- and the man who ended it, who plunged the knife in my back when he saw the opportunity. He saw in me a threat. He knew well enough I was just one step behind him, my stiletto in my waist band, waiting for any opportunity that might present itself for me to be the killer.

It's easy to me to see where all this stuff comes from. It comes from the reality, through the imagination, back around to the reality. It's a giant, circular flow.

As I get older, this becomes so much clearer to me. It wouldn't be clear yet to young Deuteronomy Jackson or to Chaqueena, his bitch, my brilliant college student. But when I imagined them into the future...

28

Let us imagine together, then, the entrance of the Shake-spearean Deuteronomy Jackson, the black Shylock, and his most exquisite bitch Chaqueena into the mobile home where Tony Jones was bound in a straight-backed chair. Chaqueena in a thin, wife-beater tee-shirt, with no bra underneath, so that her breasts were constrained only by the diaphanous fabric.

This would be all Tony Jones really cared about at this moment where his existence was soon to end, as it will soon end for all of us, in unimaginable suffering and fear and inevitability.

In that inescapable reality, what will any of us have at our disposal but to latch on to some thought of indescribable, sublime beauty?

This is where we inevitably have to go, isn't it? As the reality of our existence becomes the inevitability of our unreality, we must go where Shakespeare always takes us, to the turn of phrase, the flight of poetry, the sublimity of character, the glimpse of the immortal that confronts us everywhere in his work.

Let's go now with Tony. Our balls are going to be sliced off by our arch-enemy, our doppel-ganger, the man we love so much because we see ourselves in him. And he is going to be assisted by our love-goddess. We are going to be sacrificed to beauty and to, what? What else are we going to die for? It's so attractive. The pull is so strong.

29

Tony must meet his destiny mute. He has the rubber ball taped in his mouth. He can only talk with his eyes.

He must communicate his love with his eyes. Chaqueena needs to know how he feels, now that it is almost over. He cannot hide any more. She has to see his longing, his admiration, his worship.

And Deuteronomy has to see it. He has to see the thing he didn't really expect- Tony's love for him. Because yes, Tony loves him now, now that the bastard is going to kill him, horribly and painfully.

Tony can't help but love him. Deuteronomy is so like himself. But Deuteronomy goes that extra place where Tony never dared to go. Now Tony was going to visit it with his whole being, with his entire existence.

To lose his balls while Chaqueena watched. To bleed here silently to death. Tis a consummation devoutly to be wished.

To die. To sleep, no more. To sleep, no more to dream, for when he shuffled off this mortal coil, no dreams would come, as they had for so many months, dreams in which he loved Chaqueena and she loved him, drawing his loins into her lusciousness, kissing his mouth with her softness, giving everything he had ever truly needed.

Why was she the goddess of his dreams? What made her that? From what mansion of the sublime did she issue forth, flesh and blood, evanescence and personality? Dream and reality in one. Surpassing imagination. Surpassing language. Surpassing reality itself and taking him into the place beyond it. The one that is so much more true in every way.

Enough. *We have some details to attend.*

30

There is the question of Portia's disguise. In The Merchant, *Portia must become a man. It is critical to the plot, because a woman could not be a lawyer in that era, and Portia must disguise herself as a lawyer to save everyone in this play.*

Our fictional Portia can't become a man.

Well, of course she can become a man these days. Literally.

But you wouldn't really believe that, would you? Not really at this point of the story. Having a surgeon give her a penis? A set of balls? Constructing it all out of the very core of her femininity? Sure, it happens all the time, but you aren't really going to let me get away with that, are you?

Our imaginary Portia will have to disguise herself in some way as the savior. She must save Tony and everyone, even Deuteronomy, from the horrific bloodshed that is about to take place right in front of us.

You really don't want to see that happen, do you? You don't want Deuteronomy to take that bread knife and saw Tony's genitals off, as the victim writhes and screams into the rubber ball and tape. You don't want Chaqueena watching- like an Aztec princess watching sacrifices on the sacred pyramids.

You want Portia and me to save you.

Now you've got two stories going, and you really don't know how they're going to end, do you?

You're having to trust me a little.

But I'm only making one of these stories up. Kind of. I mean it was made up centuries ago. And we have certain expectations of how it is going to end.

31

Before you can go there, you need to learn a good bit more about what happened between the real Deuteronomy Jackson and me.

I felt like such a loser.

Working as a teacher. I mean. Is there any profession in our society that is less enviable? I was a boring, aged-out fart teaching Shakespeare, or even worse, Accounting 101, to a bunch of students from the wrong sides of town. The very wrong sides of town. The sides you never go into.

You have no idea how these people live. The crap they are caught up in. It's unbelievable. I thought I knew- back in my old life. When I lived like- how can I put it? When everyone I dealt with traveled and lived in marvelous homes and drove very nice cars and vacationed in very nice places and where the world I'm talking about now, the world from which my students come, was just a place we never drove through unless we were lost?

There I go again. I'm wandering off the point.

I was telling how I got into the trouble with the real Deuteronomy Jackson. I was a teacher. I had been reduced to utter schmuckdom. I was painfully infatuated with a brilliant, black stripper. She was toying with my affections like I was the broke, old schmuck I had become. And I wanted out. I wanted to be somebody again. I desperately wanted to be somebody.

Here was young Jackson. I saw him at school one day, coming out of a computer lab. I knew the instructor. When Deuteronomy was gone, I stuck my head in the empty lab and pretended Deuteronomy was a student of mine. It was an opening to the other instructor to gossip about him.

"He's a drug dealer, you know," I said.

The instructor was only slightly surprised. "Well," he said, "walks like a duck, quacks like a duck... It's a shame, though. The most brilliant programmer I've ever seen."

"And you know he'll drop out," I said.

Well, of course it was politically incorrect, so the other instructor put on the requisite airs. Or did he really believe in the kid?

Jackson. Oh, that magnificent bastard. How he could play us all. He could fire the imagination and the desire. He was a hope merchant.

32

It was in Chaqueena's apartment that I really saw that side of him.

What the hell was I doing in Chaqueena's apartment?

I was there to get laid. This unimaginable affair was going to be my first foray into full-blown infidelity. Oh, God, how I leaped across a canyon to get there.

Chaqueena was in my office in school, a few weeks after the incident in the school library- a week or two after my visit to the strip club. She was talking about her career plans. She wanted to go to medical school, she said. I was trying to be a good professor, a good mentor. I was talking her through the plans and the possibilities as realistically as I could...

Then she told me what she wanted to specialize in.

"I really want to study sex," she said, with a mischievous smile. "Is there a specialty, like- what would you call it- sexology?"

Her skirt barely covered her underwear as she sat in front of my desk, her strong legs crossed demurely. A vest-like blouse was tucked tight around her breasts and her waistline.

I don't know what pushed me over that canyon, out into the open air, with nothing underneath me, but I said it. I didn't just blurt it out. I thought about it, weighed the consequences, and said it.

"Chaqueena," I said, lowering my voice so no one could possibly hear me through the thin walls of the adjoining faculty offices, "I want to make love to you. I want to have sex with you."

She sat there smiling. For a long time. For a long, long time when I thought my heart was going to stop.. I was going to collapse into cardiac arrest on the floor.

"I want to fuck you, too, Evan," she said.

I couldn't speak. I couldn't breathe.

"I want you to fuck me. I want you to do me in my apartment," she said.

I sucked in my breath as if someone had punched me.

"Can you imagine doing that, Evan?" she said.

"Vividly," I said.

"Well, Evan," Chaqueena said. "Sounds like we need to go there. Because I don't think your wife is going to want you to fuck me at your house."

33

She gave me her address. I entered it into my cell phone. She was going to leave ten minutes ahead of me. I was going to follow in my car. Nobody would associate our movements.

I was sweating. I exuded guilt. I exuded lust.

How did she know it would do to me what it did? Any remnant of reason was gone- any trace of self-control vanished. I was a man on a primordial mission.

Imagine it? Oh my Lord. I lived it- for the entire ten minutes I waited after she left my office, for the three minutes or so it took me to scratch a note canceling office hours, fumble with the lock, look with astonishing guilt up and down the hallway to see if anyone was watching, dash down the stairwell and out to my car. Then for the twenty minutes it took me to drive to her apartment, following the voice on Google Maps- half listening- making three wrong turns.

All this time I was imagining so vividly the anatomical details, the hygiene details, the fears about how long I would last, the comparisons with Deuteronomy Jackson. With Deuteronomy's much more virile, and (in my imagination) enormously larger penis. I had trouble breathing.

Then I was there, in the parking lot of a run-of-the-mill apartment complex. Chaqueena's apartment was on the second floor. I didn't even check to see if anyone was watching. I wouldn't know anybody here. Not on this side of town.

I took the stairs two at a time. I knocked on her door.

She came to the door in all her glory. Naked.

She took me by the hand and pulled me into her apartment.

34

Portia, if we are going to continue to the follow the Shake-spearean model, will have to use both a transsexual disguise and a brilliant legal argument to free Tony from his predica-ment. How, you may wonder, am I going to pull that off?

Well, what about this?

Portia disguises herself as a transsexual.

Yes, she should appear to be transsexual. She should be one of those women who look so much like men you begin to believe they are. Before the hormone injections and the surgery begins. Before the voice gets really low and the beard begins to grow. Before the breasts are cut off. Before the construction of the pe-nis and scrotum begins. We've all seen them now. They are in our workplaces. They are in the stores. They are in my classes.

We may, in fact, know them far more intimately.

What must it feel like? *I am beginning to know. You, though, probably have no idea what confusion this creates. So much of us depends on sex. At least in our society. It's the defin-ing thing, isn't it? It's more defining than race.*

Unfortunately, like race, it's a completely imaginary dis-tinction that begins to break down seriously on the margins. Black blends into white across a phalanx of mixed-race chil-dren, a generation or two nowadays where the procreating, young public don't really give a damn about black and white any more.

The same thing is happening with sexes. My students don't blink when the transsexual girl or boy speaks up in class- when you call the roll and realize for the first time they really aren't at all what you expected they are.

My colleague in the office next door, a young lesbian, came to me the other day, before the semester started, with an email from a student who identified herself as a man. The student was asking her professor to use a man's name, not her female name on the class role, to identify her at the beginning of class.

Old codger that I am, I felt genuine human compassion for this young man, or young woman, or...

But my young, lesbian colleague had no sympathy whatsoever. "This just means she," she said. (Did she say "she" or "he"? I can't remember.) "This just means he doesn't really know what he is," she said. "He really hasn't made the commitment yet, and she's fishing for a reaction from me. She's not comfortable in her own skin."

Portia Stephens was comfortable in her own skin- preternaturally so. And her own skin is what she wore to her meeting with Deuteronomy Jackson. She cut her hair like a man's. She bought a man's clothes. But she was wearing her own skin under that pinstriped, black suit, white shirt, and tightly knotted, power tie when she walked into the front door of Deuteronomy Jackson's office building in North Charlotte. She was clutching a leather brief. Nerissa followed right behind her.

No one greeted them when they entered the small waiting room. No one came to the reception window.

Portia pushed the intercom button and announced herself.

"Mel Patterson to see Deuteronomy Jackson," she said. There was a long silence. The lock on the entry door buzzed.

35

They met Deuteronomy Jackson *(the imaginary one)* just inside the armored security door, in the dark, empty space that used to be a grocery store.

He shook their hands, introduced himself, and led them to his inner sanctum.

They were amazed, as were all of Jackson's guests on their first visit to this place, but you've already gone there before. You've already formed your picture of how it all looked.

When they were seated, Portia began to talk.

"Mr. Jackson," she said, "I'm not going to mince words. I believe you have kidnapped my client, and you are holding him for ransom at this moment. Since the FBI considers all kidnapping victims to have been transported across state lines, this crime will be considered *prima facie* a federal offense when I report it to them. I will report the crime to the FBI, with you as primary suspect, one hour from now, unless Tony Jones reappears at his home in Charlotte, unharmed and in good health."

Deuteronomy just stared at her. He stared long enough that Portia began to rise from her chair.

"Damn," Deuteronomy said, "you a chick."

Portia stared back at him.

"I mean I thought you was a guy," Deuteronomy said in amazement. "I mean a little scrawny, pussy guy."

"Fuck you," Portia said. She rose to her full height.

"But you got you a set of balls," Deuteronomy said, chuckling. "Hey, I bet you ain't even got any balls, is you?"

"Come on," Portia said to Nerissa. "This asshole has fifty-nine minutes left. And it's going to take him a while to figure this out." She laid a business card on Deuteronomy's desk.

"Hey!" Deuteronomy said, captivated by a thought, "I bet you one of those chicks with a dick." He was genuinely interested. "You know, like you see in the back of Hustler magazine."

"I am," Portia said, "a man. As if that were any of your business."

"Yeh, you look like you one of those chicks with a dick," Deuteronomy said. "You know they's people really born that way. Got a pussy. Got a dick. Both of them. Shit, go on the damn internet. You can see em- fuckin and suckin each other."

"Let's go," Portia said to Nerissa.

"What the hell you mean coming in my office with this bullshit?" Deuteronomy roared. He stood and shouted. "Do you know who the hell I am? Do you know who you're dealing with?"

He picked up her card and read it.

"Stinson, Montgomery?" he said. "I'll call Lewis Stinson right now. You sit your skinny, no-balls ass down while I call him. This is the end of your fucking law career, missy, or mister, or whatever the fuck you are."

Portia did not sit. "Go ahead and call him," she said.

Deuteronomy did just that.

The founding partner of Charlotte's most prestigious law firm informed him Mel Patterson was indeed representing Tony Jones in this matter. Jackson would be well-advised to listen carefully to whatever Mr. Patterson had to say, the founding partner suggested.

36

"So what you're telling me," Deuteronomy said, when he and Portia were seated again, "is that your client has such a clean conscience about his own recent business dealings that he would welcome an inquiry from the FBI into this case?"

"My client is one of the most respected business leaders in this state," Portia said.

"He's a drug smuggler," Deuteronomy said. "Did he ever tell you about that?"

Portia was caught a bit off guard. It was just the slightest reaction. Not many people would have noticed it, but a man like Deuteronomy would.

"Yeh," Deuteronomy said. "And you ain't got no balls down there yet, do you? What, they gonna add you some when you have your surgery? Where they get your new balls when they do that?"

"Mr. Jackson," Portia said, "do yourself a favor and try to focus on something besides my genitalia. I can assure you I'm not thinking at all about yours."

"I don't know where the fuck Tony Jones is," Deuteronomy said. "And I don't care. Why don't you call him up and ask him? Call him up and say, 'Hey, Tony. Your good, black friend Deuteronomy Jackson said you personally smuggled eight-million-dollars worth of cocaine into the Port of Miami back in Jan-uary, and he was wondering if you want me to call the FBI in so they can investigate.'"

Portia said, "Now that you've brought up money, I'm in-structed to tell you we can deliver full payment for his debt to you this afternoon. The funds are ready to be wired to whatever account you instruct."

"Mr. Jones has already defaulted on his note," Jackson said. "We just foreclosing on our collateral."

"Why?" Portia said. And there was a silence. "It doesn't make any sense. You will be repaid in full, with interest."

"Why?" Jackson said. "Why do the police shoot unarmed black men here in Charlotte?"

Portia stared at him.

"You see when the police shoot a nigger," Deuteronomy said, "when that white homeowner shoots a nigger- when they throw that young man in prison for the same damn thing you and all your buddies did when you were all young- what the hell do you think that's about? You think that's about something rational?"

"I don't follow you," Portia said. "We're talking about a busi-ness transaction here. You will be made whole this afternoon."

"Made whole? You're going to fucking make me whole? You can't do that, Missy, or Mister, or whatever the fuck you are."

Portia said nothing.

"I'm talking to you like you're some kind of... Some kind of... What the hell am I trying to tell you?" Jackson said, "Like you ain't a goddamn person. Like you don't even fucking count, but let me tell you, you still there in your suit with your fucking law degree, and you're still white, bitch. You still don't have any fucking idea what I'm talking about."

"Mr. Jackson," Portia said, "I believe I do. I understand the injustice..."

"Understand the injustice!" Deuteronomy roared. He slammed his fists on this desk and rose to his feet. And he did something Portia never would have expected. His voice broke.

He choked back a sob.

"You," he began. He steadied himself. "You have no idea. You have no idea what Tony Jones and you and your type have been doing all your lives. You have no fucking idea. You don't even know you're doing it, do you?"

There was a long silence here. Portia didn't answer him.

"I'm not going to kill Tony Jones," Deuteronomy said. "But Tony Jones might end up having a little elective surgery, while he takes some time off to consider his financial situation."

Portia said nothing.

"Tell me," Deuteronomy said. "What's it like to be white and have no balls?"

"I am authorized to pay you twice the amount Tony Jones owed you," Portia said.

"I don't want your fucking money, bitch," Deuteronomy said. "Get out of here and leave me alone."

"Did you hear me? Twice what you are owed."

"Fuck you," Deuteronomy said.

"You'll never get away with this," Portia said. "You've got to know that."

"You have no idea what I can get away with," Jackson said. "You have no idea." He opened a small drawer and pulled out a Glock 26. He walked around the desk, walked right up to Portia, and stuck the barrel of the pistol up against her lips

She gasped, and the pistol entered her open mouth.

"You have no idea, bitch," he said.

215

37

Back to reality: Chaqueena greeted me at her apartment door- naked- and pulled me inside.

"Evan," she said. She wrapped her arms around me and kissed me, open-mouthed. I kissed her back, passionately.

She led me into her bedroom.

Here, in reality, Chaqueena's bedroom was furnished with the cheap furniture and clutter that might belong to a poor teenager. Her apartment smelled of fried food. It smelled like black people.

Chaqueena looked different here in the light of day, naked, in her own little bedroom. She had some facial hair. Not too much, but just enough to notice, and a bit of cellulite on her hips.

She reached for my belt, undid it, and unzipped my pants.

I noticed the part in her hair as she knelt in front of me- the kinky, black hair on the brown scalp.

I was erect. Fully erect. She kissed it. And she took it into her mouth.

I remember the bedspread. The cheap, polyester bedspread with little balls of worn polyester on it.

38

My real, erect penis was sliding in and out of Chaqueena's very real mouth. That mouth was an irrefutably real and integral part of her real and very beautiful, and now, I must admit, as I remember that moment- childish-looking face. So young. So childish. Like I was a child molester.

The motion of her tongue on my real erection was having the effect of making me focus on the here and the now and the nothing else but the very real, involuntary reaction I was about to have.

I moaned.

She stopped sucking. She held my scrotum cupped gently in her hand and smiled up at me.

She kissed the head of my erection, and she slid it back into her mouth.

I closed my eyes and began to thrust my hips into her.

"Yes, Chaqueena," I said.

She hummed lightly. The sensation- it was beyond words.

"You're a good cocksucker, Chaqueena," I said.

She hummed.

"I'm going to come," I said.

With a spectacular crash, the door flung open behind me.

I spun to face it.

There was Deuteronomy Jackson. The very, very real Deuteronomy Jackson.

And my involuntary reaction took place involuntarily right in front of him, with the lovely, childish Chaqueena kneeling beside me.

My seed spewed forth onto the worn, shag carpeting.

And Deuteronomy recorded video with his cell phone.

This was oh so real. And oh so right there. And the real me was the real star of it all.

39

Why do I feel the need to intersperse a fantasy story with this real history? In my last book, I wrote a novel about a real, historical figure. I interspersed that real story with a fictional story about a community college student who falls in love with his professor's niece.

At the book launch, I told the audience about a young student of mine who had inspired me. Then I admitted that I had built a fictional, modern story from the seed- nothing more than the seed, really- of that interaction with a real student. The fictional character was nothing like the real. He just started out from that one, brief incident- that bit of an idea.

One of my friends told me later he had been disappointed to hear that. When he first suspected the book was based on a real story, he said, he couldn't wait to read it. But when he found out it was fiction, he lost interest. He only likes to read true stories, he said.

This is a trend in literature today. People buy non-fiction stories written as if they were novels. But really, what's the trick in that? We have a test case laid out for you here. Which story is more interesting- the real story of my tawdry affair with the stripper/student Chaqueena, or the imaginary story of Tony Jones's affair with Chaqueena?

The real story of that dirt ball Deuteronomy Jackson video-ing my ejaculation in Chaqueena's dirty, smelly apartment?

Or the imaginary story of the multimillionaire Deuteronomy Jackson in front of Tony Jones with a bread knife?

The imaginary Chaqueena- *without the touches of reality I shared with you at the real Chaqueena's apartment?*

The imaginary Chaqueena reaching for Tony Jones's private parts, taking them in her delicate, brown fingers, pulling Tony Jones by those parts across the slick, cold seat of the straight-backed chair? The imaginary ringing of the imaginary cell phone? The imaginary words of the imaginary Deuteronomy as he reached for the phone, "What the fuck does that bitch want now?"

Which of these stories is drawing you forward? Which one will take you to the climax? Which one makes you want it more?

Hmmmmmmm....

Which one do you like better? Can you feel it down there?

Hmmmmmmm...

40

The quality of mercy is not strain'd,
It droppeth as the gentle rain from heaven
Upon the place beneath: it is twice blest;
It blesseth him that gives and him that takes:

Thus spake Portia. The Shakespearian one.

Our Portia- *our imaginary one*, was dressed as a man again. She had asked Deuteronomy to meet her at the Apex Club, in a private dining room with two doors, but no windows. No one could see them. And she spoke like this:

"Deuteronomy," she said, "I have come here to beg for mercy."

Deuteronomy winced.

"Mercy is the most important thing in the universe, Deuteronomy. It is the voice and soul of the Almighty. If you want to put it another way, and if this makes any sense to you, I think it may be the ultimate mystery of the universe."

She paused.

"The ultimate mystery of the universe?" Deuteronomy puzzled.

"It is that thing we hope for. The thing we pray for. The thing we are afraid we will not get from a cold and cruel universe. It's that thing you're really afraid to let yourself believe in, because you fear it might not come. Yet often it does come, out of nowhere. Undeserved."

"Why the fuck is a lawyer dragging me in here talking about this kind of shit?" Deuteronomy said.

"My job is my job," Portia said, gently. She approached Deuteronomy and stared in his eyes gently. "But I'm not here just to do my job."

She took one of his hands by the fingertips.

"You should spare Tony Jones," she said, "because it's the right thing to do. And I can see you have the power to do it. I can see it in you."

Deuteronomy did not take his hand away. He did not step back.

"We could have had this discussion on your cell phone," Portia said. "I didn't need to bring you here for that. Time is short, after all."

Deuteronomy did not move. She laced her fingers into his.

"I asked you here," Portia said, "because I couldn't help it. It is a mystery to me."

She kissed him. Her tongue slid into his mouth. He took her in his arms and kissed her back strongly and passionately.

And then he stepped back. He stepped back across the room.

He stared at her crotch.

"Jesus," he said.

"Be open to the mystery, Deuteronomy," she said, rearranging her trousers in the front. "Be open to what the universe is raining on you."

"Jesus," he said.

He reached for the door.

He opened the door and stumbled into the hallway outside.

He turned and stared again at her crotch.

"I ain't gonna fuck no chick with no dick," he said.

He drew in a deep breath, and then he added, with the most profound and considered judgment:

"And I don't give a damn bout no ultimate mystery of no universe."

41

I set out to tell you a straightforward fiction, a pastiche of The Merchant of Venice, *in a Tolstoyan, third-person, omniscient voice. I really wasn't going to interfere. I wasn't going to tell you a thing about myself, except in that very veiled sort of way fiction writers always do.*

Creating art out of real life is supposed to liberate us. You take the horrible, you re-imagine it, you relive it, and the horror kind of goes away.

But why, then, have I been bleeding my real life into this story? Why make these terrible confessions? Why not just veil it in fiction?

If I'm going to be honest with you, I've even been veiling the real life story. You see, it really didn't happen that way. I'm leaving out the most interesting part.

I've been leaving it out because I just don't really know how to introduce it.

I'm afraid you won't believe me. You'll find my story so strange, so far from what you're comfortable imagining, that you'll just give up on me. You won't go along if I tell the whole truth, I fear.

Truth is very hard to face. Sometimes it's hard for us to see-literally.

We often just ignore it or tell ourselves some fiction to evade it. How often do we stare straight at the truth and then come up with an elaborate self-deception to replace it?

I'm trying to take you into this gently. Perhaps if I ease you into it, you won't go away. Maybe you'll stay with me and face up to the truth I witnessed. I can only pray that you will, because I need to take someone there with me.

Please don't leave me now. Please go just a bit farther.

The truth never hurt...

Well, that's bullshit. It hurts people all the time.

42

I told you about going to Chaqueena's strip club a while back- the real Chaqueena's real strip club. But I didn't tell you the whole story.

You see it happened pretty much the way I described when I first walked into the place. Chaqueena recognized me. She called me over to the stage. She was beautiful. She was breath-takingly beautiful. She was more beautiful than I can find words to express.

And she was naked. But she wasn't altogether naked as I said earlier.

She was wearing a g-string.

And I told you the story before far too simply. I cast myself as a lecherous old man. I cast Chaqueena as an incredibly sexy, delightfully cheeky young woman.

But that was a vast oversimplification. Because...

It all happened just the way I told you earlier, except near the end of her dancing, when the announcer on the loud-speaker said, "Gentlemen, let's hear it for the lovely Miss Chaqueena!"

Deuteronomy and his friend whistled and cheered loudly. Chaqueena seemed proud and happy. Maybe it was proud and happy... Or was it more like...

What?

Like a child who had been hiding some terrible secret, and now she was sharing the secret.

She was sharing it with ... Whom?

Was she sharing it with the Man?

What the hell am I trying to get at? I'm still so confused by it all.

I applauded. I applauded heartily and tried to smile as genuinely as I could.

"That's right," the announcer said, "Miss Chaqueena! The chick with the dick."

I didn't know what I was hearing.

Deuteronomy and his friend hooted and cheered as if they were at a Carolina Panthers game.

The bartenders and the other strippers cheered and clapped. They chanted her name:

"Chaqueena! Chaqueena!"

Chaqueena danced to the end of the stage near me. She was so happy. She was so proud. She was so beautiful.

But she was so afraid. She was so vulnerable.

She was such a child. She was such a woman.

She was looking only at me.

She was looking only into my eyes, with a trust that I had never seen from any of my students. Ever.

"Are you going to show us that big dick of yours, Chaqueena?" the announcer said.

My head was spinning.

"It ain't that big," Chaqueena said, "but it sure is pretty."

I looked at the g-string. I couldn't help it. And I began to see.

But by this time her fingers were under the strings, and she was starting to slip them down her thighs.

I couldn't breathe.

She unveiled it. She showed me a lovely, waxed vagina.

And coming out of the top, emerging from her labia, was a perfectly formed, very real penis.

Just a little bit smaller than mine.

43

If you Google "ambiguous genitalia," you'll get all kinds of medical information and Intersex advocacy. If you flip over to the "Images" tab on Google, you'll see photographs and diagrams, all pretty much aimed at real people facing a very difficult life situation. You don't have to exercise your imagination too much to understand what the issues are.

You're an expectant mother or an expectant father. You've been through one of the most profound moments of your life- the birth of your child. You've just seen your precious newborn for the first time, and, in an instant, you are in a reality you never imagined. You may not even have known this particular reality existed.

Who truly knows how many births occur with ambiguous genitalia? From the reading I've done, this area of statistic-gathering seems to be rife with agendas. Whether we take the commonly promulgated figure of one in every two-thousand births, or even if we take the far more conservative, but equally plausible, figure of one in every hundred-thousand births, the inescapable truth is that a hell of a lot of people enter this ultimately mysterious universe with ambiguous genitalia.

You can ask yourself why. You are unlikely to be answered directly.

Perhaps you need to put this book down and do a bit of Googling.

Go ahead.

I'm afraid that won't get you to what I saw in that strip club, just a bit above eye level, at the level where those things are displayed in a strip club.

If you want to imagine what I saw, and if you are somewhere where you can Google without your boss or your spouse or your children ever seeing what you've been looking at, try Googling, "huge clits."

That will take you closer. Go on. Flip over to the "Images" tab. You don't have to click on the images. You won't pick up any viruses, maybe, if you stop yourself right here. You can just scroll down through the thumbnails. Hundreds of them. You'll begin to get the idea.

But you won't entirely get it. Because apparently, at least as of this writing, no woman with an enlarged clitoris quite as enlarged and quite as perfectly formed, quite as shockingly penis-like, as Chaqueena's, has taken up work in the porn industry.

Ambiguous genitalia, you may have learned by now- if you took the time to Google and read and you weren't too squeamish to dig in and see the reality- ambiguous genitalia can take many different forms and be caused by a number of different medical issues.

Is "issues" the right word?

Chaqueena, I was to find out later, had a condition called an enlarged clitoris. Although the clitoris had been prominent since birth, nobody actually talked about it until she reached puberty.

Around the time the pretty little girl started developing into the breathtakingly beautiful, vivacious woman, she also began growing what looked like a circumcised, brown penis emerging from her labia.

Everything else about her was female. Exceedingly female. Divinely female. Ineffably female.

She told me this in that conversation in my office, the one I told you about earlier, where she said she wanted to go to medical school to become a sexologist.

Maybe you understand a little better now.

I am wrestling mightily with this ultimate mystery of the universe. I am wrestling.

44

When I blurted out in my office so crudely that I wanted to have sex with Chaqueena, and when I followed her to her apartment, I knew this terrific piece of information. I knew all about it.

So in reality, Chaqueena was in my office talking with a deeply trusted, much older man. Her intellectual mentor. The man she had entrusted with her deepest secret.

She was beaming with openness and love. I had seen her in her entirety. She knew I knew.

"You the only one who's come and looked at me for what I am, Evan," she told me. "All the rest of them, they're in there to see a sex freak. You ought to see how they act and how they talk to me."

"Oh, Chaqueena," I said.

She said nothing. She frowned.

"That must hurt you terribly," I said.

And the tears just spurted out of her eyes. I've never seen tears spurt out like that.

They rolled down her young, brown cheeks. She fought back the crying. But she couldn't stop the tears.

I started to cry. Sitting behind my stupid fucking professor desk.

"I'm sorry," I said.

She nodded.

She wiped her cheeks with the back of her hands.

"I'm glad you shared your secret with me, Chaqueena," I said.

She smiled.

"You are very beautiful," I said. "Chaqueena, you're the most beautiful woman I've ever seen."

And that's how the conversation started where she told me all about her life, about her interest in going to medical school, and her interest in studying Sexology. We must have talked for a couple of hours. It was the deepest conversation I've ever had with a student. It may have been the deepest, most honest conversation I've ever had with anyone.

Time stopped, and we entered into some other dimension- where fear and judgment were overcome by love and mercy.

And then- I told her I wanted to fuck her.

45

When she came to the door of her apartment naked, she was just as beautiful as you have imagined her, but she had a penis sticking out, also.

And when she took me into her bedroom, I'm not lying when I tell you all the details I remember that made her so much more real, so much more human. But I am lying a bit about the sex act that took place between us.

And this is the lie:

I kind of hate to go back there. It's a bit pornographic, but I left out one very important detail.

You see, in the middle of the act of fellatio- Chaqueena stopped fellating, as I described earlier. She looked up to smile at me. She cupped my gonads so gently, so beautifully in her hand. And I saw what she was doing with her other hand.

She was masturbating her penis. It had swollen with excitement. It was perhaps two-thirds the length of mine at the moment.

Oh, who the hell can remember the relative sizes? I'm just trying to tell the truth the best I can.

So when Deuteronomy Jackson burst in to take his video... Well, you can imagine...

46

When Jesus appeared to St. Faustina, as he did many times, he told her the universe was governed by two rays of light that shone forth from his breast. The rays of light were mercy and hope.

I'm not making this up.

St. Faustina was an unheralded Polish nun who died in the 1930's. Jesus appeared regularly to her during her lifetime. She didn't tell anyone, but she kept a diary. She wrote it down, the way I write all this down. Some sixty years later, Pope John Paul II named Faustina a saint. He proclaimed the Sunday after Easter as Mercy Sunday, in celebration of Jesus' revelations to her.

You've probably seen images of Jesus with the rays of hope and mercy emanating from his sacred heart. They're everywhere now, on billboards, on posters. You see the images on little prayer cards and prints hanging in people's offices, for God's sake.

Assuming that Jesus wasn't lying when he appeared to St. Faustina, and assuming St. Faustina wasn't lying when she shared this story, we can conclude that William Shakespeare was writing about one of the two most important forces in the universe when he wrote a play about mercy.

I project a slide on the screen for my students after they have watched The Merchant of Venice. *This is the slide:*

> This play is about Jesus.
>> a. true
>> b. false

They have to vote on the correct answer. Then they have to defend their vote.

Most of them vote "false." No, they say, the play is about prejudice. The play is about mercy. The play is about the law. The play is about love. The play is about money.

It isn't about Jesus, they tell me.

But what do you do with Antonio? I ask. What is Antonio doing by the fourth act of the play?

If you're a bit lost here, think of what Tony Jones is doing. Tony is about to sacrifice his life, in the most barbaric and horrific way imaginable, in order to pay the debts of his brother.

47

I cannot get the image of Chaqueena's penis out of my mind.

It wasn't really a penis. It was a clitoris. It was just as sensitive as any other clitoris, according to Chaqueena. But it had no reproductive function other than as a pleasure-seeking organ.

Her vagina and urethra fulfilled the normal functions of reproduction and purgation.

It's a bit much, I know, but you do want to know, don't you?

You might also want to know how Portia's genitals were constructed. I mean the fictional one in this story, not Shakespeare's Portia. And not Portia, my real-life wife.

Let's go analytically through this, to keep it all straight.

First, there's Portia, my real wife: It may seem entirely inappropriate to be talking about my wife's sexual organs here, but we've talked about many other people's, including my own, so why not?

Portia's sexual organs are, as far as I can tell, quite normal. That is, they match, more or less, the real-life vaginas I saw and/or had some interaction with before I married her many decades ago. Hers matched more or less most of the vaginas I have seen in magazines or videos or strip clubs over the years.

It had a... well, I may be getting deeper into this than you really want me to go.

Shakespeare's Portia, on the other hand, is a different story altogether. As you probably know, Shakespeare's Portia didn't have a vagina at all. She had a penis. And a pair of fuzzy-downed balls.

She was played by a boy whose voice had not yet changed. This boy would have portrayed one of the most beautiful and alluring women in all of fiction.

Also, as would all the boys playing female characters in The Merchant of Venice, he would at one point act the role of a woman disguising herself as a young man.

How would he do this? Would he be able to lower his voice convincingly? Would he put on a false beard? Would he just change clothes?

You've heard this before, but if you think about it at all, just beyond the surface, just beyond what your high-school English teacher told you, this play would have been exceedingly difficult to pull off with boy actors playing the female parts.

Why does Shakespeare have all the women dress up as men? Why would the male characters seem to express their most passionate interest and admiration toward these characters when they are dressed as men?

You are not the first to wonder.

48

We've discussed the genital appearance of my wife and Shakespeare's Portia. What about the fictional Portia of our story?

Maybe you see this coming. Lovely Portia Stephens. The billionairess. Why would her father put in place his labyrinthine and nefarious will? Why would he construct that trap for her suitors? Why would he try to bind them into that relationship with his vast wealth and power?

He loved Portia. We've established that. She loved him. And his will worked, didn't it? She married Bass Jones, and they appear to have been happy and sexually active in the months leading up to her marriage. Portia seems to have formed her first long-term commitment.

As you have certainly guessed by now, even though Portia was beautiful, wise, and wealthy, and she had that special thing that Portias have in this story, she also had that other special thing.

She had a thing just like Chaqueena's. The real Chaqueena.

Portia's was only slightly smaller than Bass's. I'm sure you really don't want the details, but you've got to know enough to put this into perspective. When Portia gets excited, that thing is swollen and it's, well, large.

Bass loves Portia. He sees her for all she is.

It doesn't hurt that she's got a billion dollars to share with him. A man can get cozy with a lot of things for a billion dollars. He can put it in his mouth. He can let her... You don't really want me to go there, do you?

Why don't you just go there yourself in your imagination? No need for me to take you there.

Just let your imagination wander...

49

So what did the real Deuteronomy Jackson do with his video of me and the real Chaqueena? Well, he had some considerable leverage over me as of that moment.

You can see perhaps how I wound up as an employee of Deuteronomy Jackson over the next few years. I was a white man, a former leading businessman in the community, now a mild-mannered college professor, and I had a forty-foot sailboat that I took every summer to the Bahamas.

Why did I have a sailboat again, you may ask?

Because I was beginning to have some money, goddamnit. I had money because Deuteronomy paid me sixty-thousand dollars a delivery.

I hated Deuteronomy Jackson. I hated what he was doing to me. I loved Chaqueena.

I liked my new boat.

I could never really get over her. I could never get her out of my mind. Whenever I saw her, she was with him, and it was clear I was never going to go back to that moment of physical love- the special thing I had never imagined and never experienced anywhere else.

I did six summers of drug running- most of it from the Out Islands of the Bahamas up to the Carolinas coast. Easy peasy. I

*cleared customs every time I did it. Called in to the Customs hot
line like I was supposed to. Took my crew with me up to the
nearest customs office with our passports.*

*The customs officers never inspected my boat. I offloaded
my payload after all my crew went home. I was reputable,
white, boring as hell, and anonymous. The customs people
didn't give a damn about me. People like Deuteronomy Jackson smuggled drugs. I just went boating.*

*Then he wanted me to start delivering up to the Northeast.
That's what I really hated. He had me running in late May or
early June from the Bahamas all the way up to his house in
Martha's Vineyard. Yes, that damn mansion on the bluff overlooking the harbor in Edgartown. What the hell was a thug like
him doing with that place? Five years after I met him in that
sleazy strip club in Charlotte? Damnit, how upside down is the
world when Deuteronomy Jackson and his stripper girlfriend
own a mansion in Edgartown, and I, a college-educated, for-
mer-CFO am running drugs up to him and offloading them on
his dock?*

*I hated the run up to Edgartown. That time of year the
weather hasn't really begun to settle for the summer, and the
Gulf Stream becomes monstrous when the Northers blow
through. It scared the crap out of me. Twenty-foot seas off
Hatteras. The boat would leap off the tops of the waves and
crash in the troughs. Spray blew over me in sheets.*

*I was scared and cold and seasick. I had no damn choice. I
was a thrall.*

50

I'm sorry. I'm trying to keep three stories going at once. I bet you're getting tired as the reader.

So- just a quick little recap- sort of like those recaps that let the watchers of television series skip over the episodes they missed and jump back into the middle of the story.

Shakespeare: *Shylock has taken Antonio to court and demands his pound of flesh, a certain death sentence for Antonio. Portia disguises herself as a male lawyer and shows up in court to defend Antonio.*

Our fiction: Deuteronomy Jackson has kidnapped Tony Jones and plans to cut off his genitals. Portia has disguised herself as a lawyer in an attempt to defend Tony. Portia is pretending to be an Intersex lawyer. Or a lawyer with ambiguous genitalia. She's only pretending about the lawyer part of that.

Our reality: *You have now discovered my true story of infidelity with my Intersex undergraduate. You have seen how I was blackmailed by that motherfucker, the real Deuteronomy Jackson, into years of drug running between the Bahamas and the United States. I told myself I did it because I was being blackmailed.*

243

But now I know I was doing it because I hated myself. I hated myself as the man who had tried to screw Chaqueena, the one person I had ever really been honest with.

Deuteronomy had caught me at that, and he used it. He used me like I had intended to use Chaqueena.

As much as I resented it, though, it did make my summer employment far more lucrative than my employment the rest of the year as a college professor.

To catch up with the other two stories, I'm going to have to tell you how I wound up kidnapped by Deuteronomy and how Chaqueena came to be holding my testicles in one hand and a sharp knife in the other. I will also tell how my Portia, my real Portia, came to my rescue.

51

Deuteronomy was so much like the CEO of our company, the company I worked for back in the unimaginable past when I was a real man with a real job.

I had worked with that bastard since we were boys, right out of college.

By the time we were in our forties, we were running the place. We were the top dogs. Everyone had to roll over and stick their legs in the air and show me their balls when I growled at them. And the CEO, my supposed lifelong friend, loved to make me roll over and bare my balls to him, whenever he felt like it- whenever it humiliated me the most.

It's just what guys do, especially guys in the business world. It's the way we run things.

The best can make you roll over and yelp while they have a smile on their face and no menace in their voice.

Did you ever see President Obama do it? On the television?

You couldn't even hear the growling.

I had been trained to assume the supine position for over two decades before I met young Deuteronomy Jackson. He read me from the moment he met me. He could smell the Beta male in me all the way across Charlotte. He knew I would do his bidding, over and over, running right behind him in the pack, as his gonads flopped in the wind right in front of my nose. He knew exactly where I would run in his pack, and he knew I would run a long way.

So I delivered his dope. He paid me for one delivery run every summer, disguised as one leg of my normal, summer cruise. For that one part of my cruise, he paid me considerably more than I made as a college instructor working the other nine months of the year.

I had a pretty good life, really. I worked at a job that wasn't all that bad. I kind of liked teaching Shakespeare. And I didn't mind teaching the accounting so much.

I even got a blow job from a beautiful accounting student once.

Portia got off my back. She was pretty tough on me when we went broke. I'm surprised the marriage survived that passage. But as the years went by, and as our lives settled out after the Great Recession, she didn't mind that I seemed to have steady work. I had gotten a full-time job as an English instructor at a community college. I had health insurance. A meager pension.

Portia liked taking her summer vacations and going sailing with me. We had a lot of fun doing it. She began looking at me as a complete, functioning man again.

When Portia wasn't sailing with me, I would get some of my buddies to help move the boat between the U.S. and the Bahamas. They weren't on board when I loaded Deuteronomy's deliveries.

They weren't on board when I offloaded. They never suspected they were smuggling drugs. But they were excellent cover- boring, middle-aged, white guys with college educations, families, and solid reputations. They ran dope for Deuteronomy Jackson and never suspected it.

I didn't let Portia or any of my friends meet Deuteronomy or Chaqueena, although I did spend time with the couple every now and then.

I remember one spectacular dinner in the dining room of the Edgartown mansion, with the view I described in our fictional story earlier. Lovely Chaqueena was a gracious hostess. She wanted to discuss Shakespeare, I remember. She got me talking about the mysteries of the universe, and how that was what drew me so to Shakespeare's plays- how he could limn the ultimate mystery of the universe with words...

That's when Deuteronomy, in real life, said the thing I've always remembered:

"Man, I don't give a damn bout no ultimate mystery of no universe!"

Oh, fuck the bastard!

Having ended my lovely dinner conversation with the most beautiful woman I had ever known, he led her away and shooed me out of his mansion. He took her upstairs, no doubt, to screw her in the most unimaginable way.

What did he do with her dick, I wondered?

It didn't matter. I hated him. He had made me roll over on my back and show my balls to him one too many times. The bastard.

52

The next summer, when he told me to pick up a delivery at _____ Cay in the Exumas and deliver it back to Charleston, I resolved I was going to fuck him.

I had never looked inside the smallish packets of dope I delivered each summer. They were wrapped in brown, plastic tape, each about the size of a trade paperback novel, but with substantially more heft.

I had always been told they were cocaine. Six compartments were built into my boat underneath the false floors of storage lockers. On top of the hidden compartments, the lockers were stuffed full of boat gear- gear I let no one else pull out. I fished the gear out only to load the dope and unload it at my destination.

I was anchored in the Bahamas, having been visited this time by Deuteronomy himself driving a flat-bottomed, beat-up skiff. I was alone. Portia would fly in to Staniel Cay to meet me in two days. I had Deuteronomy's hundred-or-so pounds of contraband spread out on the berth in one of the aft cabins, preparing to stow it in the smuggling compartments.

I took one of the packets and felt it. I was planning to take five pounds of the stuff- about seventy-thousand-dollars' worth. I figured I could move it without much trouble at retail.

Seventy-thousand dollars would make life easier for Portia and me, but not so much easier that she would wonder where the extra money was coming from.

My plan was to cut five pounds out, replace it with five pounds of sugar I had specially pounded to the consistency of powdered cocaine, and deliver the packages as required. I figured I needed to open at least half the packets. Then I needed to repack them so no one could tell the difference. This was going to be an all-night operation, but I was by myself in a spectacular Exumas anchorage. What else did I have to do?

I picked up one of the packages, the so-familiar packages to me by this time, after seven summers of running Deuteronomy's dope. I began to inspect it.

This package was no different from the ones I had delivered before, was it? I wondered.

Did it have crisper, more defined edges and corners? Was it heavier and stiffer?

The wrapping job was the same- intended to defeat exactly the kind of tampering I was about to do. But I'm no dumb ass drug smuggler. I had thought this through.

I began working with tweezers and a box-cutter, like a surgeon. I carefully spread a plastic sheet on the berth to catch the cocaine that would fall out. I had my vacuum-packing machine and plastic tape ready for the repackaging.

No cocaine fell out. There was no cocaine inside the package.

Instead, there were vacuum-packed stacks of hundred-dollar bills. Used, non-sequential, hundred-dollar bills.

I wasn't smuggling dope.

I was laundering money.

Ah, a financial transaction! I thought.

Well, I knew how to manage those.

53

One-hundred pounds of hundred-dollar bills. I counted carefully through the pack. I tested its weight against the other packets. I did the arithmetic.

Five-million dollars in cash. I laughed. Only five million.

Deuteronomy Jackson didn't really need me. Five-million dollars was a lot of money for most people, but from the world I had come from- from the world I was beginning to understand Deuteronomy lived in, these packets of bills, this hundred-pounds of cold, untraceable cash, was just a transfer from savings to checking, so to speak.

I left the money lying out on the berth that night.

I didn't really sleep. I sat in the cockpit and let the tropical breeze blow my graying hair. I listened to the wavelets lap, and I thought.

I thought about all the changes in my world. I was sick and tired of having done whatever I was supposed to do for fifty-odd years. I had bought the whole, ridiculous sack of shit.

I started out as a white scion of well-to-do society. I went to segregated schools in Charlotte. I witnessed the violence over busing to integrate the schools. I wasn't in those buses myself. My family had pulled me out of public school and put me in Charlotte Latin by that time. But I remember seeing a white mob rocking a yellow school bus as our mom drove us to school.

I had gone to Vanderbilt- and to Wharton- had bought into it all. I'd worked my way up through the real estate develop-ment business.

I married Portia. I'd stuck in there. Let me tell you, that was one hell of a lot of sticking.

Poor Portia. For God's sake. I'm getting blow jobs from an Intersex undergrad as thanks for it. Now I had been running drugs for five years in a boat she had grown to love, that she thought was a symbol of our love and humility and hard work and perseverance through all the adversity we had faced in re-cent years- the adversity all of us Americans faced. The adver-sity all of us faced except Deuteronomy Jackson and the ex-CEO of our development company flying around in their god-damn private jets and staying in their homes in Edgartown and Telluride.

You know exactly how I felt. Even if you're reading this in your private jet or in your Edgartown mansion, you know how badly the rest of us have taken it in the past twenty years. Without the Vaseline.

I sat up in the cockpit and thought about all this, and I think for the first time in my life I decided to stop rolling over on my back and sticking my balls up in the air. I decided it was time to turn my life around.

The next morning, I set sail for Nassau. I still had connec-tions there. I still knew people. I knew people who could deal with a five-million-dollar cash deposit. These people could lube it and slide it into the international banking system- make it invisible. That was the easy part. The tough part was going to be telling Deuteronomy Jackson I had done it.

54

Which didn't go particularly well.

I led with my MBA from Wharton. With being the former CFO of the fifth-largest real estate development firm in the country.

I told him, in the best laid-out presentation, how I could revolutionize his cash management practices and net him, according to the spreadsheets and the pitch book I was talking him through, over a million dollars a year in returns and tax benefits.

He let me get all the way through the pitch. He looked like he was going to kill me the whole time. But he did listen to it all.

Within three hours, I was duct-taped naked in a straight-backed chair in a mobile home two hours outside of Charlotte.

I had the rubber ball taped in my mouth.

Well, you've already imagined this scene a few times already. You know what it looked like.

55

"You get a nigger gone wild like this, you gotta shoot his ass," Lancelot said as their limousine sped through the North Carolina countryside. He ejected the magazine from his Uzi.

"I mean you gotta put the muthafuckah down," he said. He pulled another banana clip from the bag at his feet and inserted it into the machine gun.

Then he began to shuck bullets from the first magazine, counting silently. His lips moved as he counted.

"Now wait a minute," Bass said. "We're coming out here to talk, right? We're out here to talk some sense into Deuteronomy. He's a businessman."

"You gonna talk to a nigger fixing to cut your brother's dick off?" Lancelot said. He lost count of the bullets in his agitation.

"You try to talk to that muthafuckah, he'll be cutting your dick off, too," Lancelot said, "and his too," he said, indicating Gray. "And specially his," pointing to Lorenzo. "White muthafuckah been fucking his daughter, for God's sake. You out of your fucking mind. We going out here to shoot us at least one nigger, and we probably fixin to shoot us three or four."

Bass didn't respond. The car sped into the autumn countryside.

There was a long silence in the car.

Lancelot restarted his bullet count. He was concentrating heavily.

56

When Portia (the real one, my wife) found out what had happened to me, she too armed herself and sped into the Carolina countryside.

She didn't have an Uzi. She had her nine-millimeter Glock.

"Portia," I had said into my cell phone when they pulled the rubber ball from my mouth and held the cell phone up to my ear.

"What do you want?" She said. She was irritated. I was interrupting something. And she had been irritated with me lately.

"Portia," I started to cry. "Portia, I love you. I'm so sorry. I'm so sorry I got into this trouble. Please believe how much I love you and how sorry I am. I never meant to get you involved."

"Shut up that crying, you pussy," Deuteronomy said. "Tell her how to get out here. Tell her I want your computer."

I had to explain my predicament to my wife while I was taped naked to a chair in a mobile home. I had to talk her into coming to my aid. I also managed to talk her into not calling the police, and without saying any words anyone else would understand, I talked her into bringing her concealed weapon.

I hoped she would be wearing a skirt, with the thigh-holster that let her hide the thing right underneath her vagina.
She figured that out herself.

57

It was amazing when Portia reached up under her short skirt and pulled it out. I thought she would start firing immediately- straight into Deuteronomy Jackson's brain, the way she had been trained to do.

Actually, in all those stupid Concealed-Carry classes we attended, I never imagined she would point that gun at anybody besides me. Ever.

But she did. She pulled it out, stuck it straight in Deuteronomy's face at a distance of about three feet, and said, in a re-markably calm voice, "Let him go, you bastard. Take whatever you want off that computer, but you let my husband go."

Chaqueena laughed.

"She gonna shoot your ass, Deuteronomy," Chaqueena said.

Deuteronomy laughed.

Deuteronomy grabbed the pistol in Portia's hand- in one motion so fluid and so quick it was almost no motion at all.

The gun fired. Twice.

The bullets shattered a window of the mobile home.

Then Deuteronomy had the gun. He had his muscular arm around Portia's neck, bending her head and shoulders toward the ground.

It takes far longer to tell you what happened than it all took to happen.

"Bitch was gonna shoot your ass, Deuteronomy," Chaqueena said.

"Shut up," Jackson said.

He dragged Portia to a chair, stuffed her into it, and held the pistol to her temple.

"Get the duct tape," he said.

58

Now, back to the fictional version of Deuteronomy Jackson and Tony Jones. You've been there half a dozen times, I realize.

Let's pan out a bit.

Look around the house trailer.

There are other people duct-taped in chairs. They are not happy, at least to the extent you can judge their expressions with rubber balls taped into their mouths.

You see, Bass's negotiation approach prevailed over Lancelot's. They tried to deal with Deuteronomy as reasonable business people. They were carrying weapons, but they didn't go in with guns blazing.

You see how it turned out.

Bass was in the chair closest to Tony, facing him. Gray was duct-taped a couple of feet to his left. Lorenzo, bleeding like Jesus from a deep gash across his forehead, was slumped against the tape that held his torso tight to the chair.

And Lancelot... Well, Lancelot was outside, recuperating from an interview with his former colleagues. The interview had not gone in his favor.

Bassanio's pants and underwear were bunched around his ankles. The other two victims had been bared for the sacrifice, also.

Chaqueena, as you have read previously, had just pulled Tony's genitals across the chair, giving Deuteronomy the "sawing room" he had demanded.

And Deuteronomy was on the phone with Portia.

"This shit is over, bitch," he said.

There was talking on the other end, but we won't be able to hear it.

"I don't give a shit what you..." Deuteronomy said.

More talking on the other end.

"Mother fucker," he said. He appeared to hang up on the telephone conversation. He immediately poked at something on his cell phone screen. Then he poked again.

Then he poked again.

And then he watched in stunned silence. For a long time.

59

I've been lying to you again.

I lied when I told you about Deuteronomy's meeting with Portia at the Apex Club.

You remember their passionate kiss.

You remember Deuteronomy's exit and his refusal to do what she was proposing.

You may remember his avidly expressed disinterest in the ultimate mystery of the universe.

That fucking bastard.

But this is what Deuteronomy wanted to remember about that incident. It is merely his imagined story. It's not what really happened.

Because what really happened was playing as a video in front of him on his cell phone.

Portia had maneuvered him so expertly in front of the camera- like the director of a pornographic video. How had he not seen this camera? How was the quality of the video so excellent, so professional?

The anatomical details were so clear. So vivid. So huge. So precise.

Deuteronomy's passion was so deep. His groaning so real.

The act of fellatio he performed was so slurpy, as Portia smiled delightedly into the camera.

Deuteronomy couldn't turn away from the video he was watching on his cell phone. He didn't care if others in the house trailer could hear the audio. They heard Deuteronomy's own, passionate cursing coming from his cell phone.

They couldn't see what was causing this cursing- how she had turned him over, onto his hands and knees, on top of the Apex Club's dining-room table. How she lubricated her fingers and began working on his rear end. How he groaned.

How she climbed onto the table behind him, when he was ready. How she mounted him and reached around.

And how he roared like a lion as his manhood dribbled onto the mahogany tabletop at Tony Jones' private club.

60

I know you don't want literary criticism right in the middle of your damn novel, but...

I admit what a racist bowl of tripe that last scene was. Just as, I'm sure, Shakespeare realized what racist tripe The Merchant of Venice *is.*

You can talk about how Shakespeare humanizes his stock villain. You can say Shakespeare makes Shylock a fully-rounded and human character, that he evokes enough sympathy for the character to redeem himself for pandering to his racist audiences.

Have I done that? Have I made the fictional Deuteronomy Jackson round enough, human enough to justify my racist portrayal of him?

Or have I just pandered to you?

But wait, you have to find out what the real Deuteronomy Jackson did to the real me, still. That may help you understand where I'm coming from.

61

We've got to clean up the mess we left on the table in the private dining room at the Apex Club.

The bottom line, I'm happy to report, is that Portia's porn video saved Tony's and Bass's and Gray's and Lorenzo's genitalia from near-certain separation.

"What you watching, Deuteronomy?" Chaqueena said in the house trailer.

Deuteronomy said nothing.

"You fucking somebody in that video," she said. "I hope you ain't fucking me."

He said nothing to her. He was transfixed.

On the video, he roared.

"Damn, somebody done stuck something up your ass," Chaqueena said. "I know that sound."

Deuteronomy had a look on his face that was far beyond words.

"Oh Jesus!" he said.

But he was talking to the ultimate mystery of the universe here.

"Oh Boo," Chaqueena said. "They ain't sent that to your Aunt Irma?"

Deuteronomy stared at her.

"Is they?" Chaqueena said.

62

At any rate, the hostages were soon untied. They were led back to their limousine. The newly freed men drove Lancelot to the hospital, where he was treated for extensive lacerations, hematomas, a concussion, and a number of cracked bones, but where he was anticipated to recover with only minimal restrictions on his activities for the remainder of his life.

Lorenzo's scalp laceration was sutured. He was released to his friends by midnight.

Portia and Nerissa met them at Tony's lovely home in Myers Park in the early morning hours.

The first thing they all noticed was Portia's new, butch haircut.

Jessica found them all on the patio. She rushed to Lorenzo when she saw his bandages.

Tony's sloping lawn stretched toward the golf course of the Myers Park Country Club. The night was amazingly dark and clear.

Lorenzo led his wife onto the lawn. She held him tightly and gently. She kissed him on the cheek.

"How sweet the moonlight sleeps upon this bank!" Lorenzo said to her, softly. "Sit, Jessica."

She sat with him on the grass.

"Look how the floor of heaven is thick inlaid with patterns of bright gold," Lorenzo said.

"What are you saying, my dear?" she said. "You sound like Shakespeare. Are you sure you don't have a concussion?"

"The reason is, your spirits are attentive," he replied. "The man that hath no music in himself, nor is not moved with concord of sweet sounds, let that man not be trusted."

Meanwhile, Bass and Tony were trying desperately to understand what had happened to them.

Jessica and Nerissa were doing their best to hinder their understanding. They were playing with them as a cat plays with a mouse.

Jessica said something like this:

"It is almost morning, and yet I am sure you are not satisfied of these events at full. Let us go in and charge us there upon interrogatories, and we will answer all things faithfully."

Bass didn't seem to hear what she said, "But what if the Pinkerton guys ever find that video?" he said, plaintively.

And Portia laughed. "You fat thing," she said. "I love you so much."

"Seriously," Bass insisted.

"Well, we'd lose all that money. But that money's not real. It's just imaginary, Bass. Just numbers out on the Internet, is all."

Bass was so puzzled.

"And what you and I have is real," said Portia. "It's the only thing that's real, isn't it? You haven't seen that yet?"

Tony laughed.

But nobody else laughed, because they were all puzzled. Instead, they went inside, where everybody went to bed.

That is the end of our fictional story.

Now on to the reality.

63

"You see," the real Deuteronomy told Portia and me, "you two motherfuckers ain't got no idea what you dealing with here."

Portia and I were duct-taped into two chairs, facing each other. I was naked. She was not.

We each had rubber balls taped into our mouths.

"Deuteronomy," Chaqueena said, "the quality of mercy is not strained. It falleth as the gentle rain from heaven."

"What the fuck is that?" he said.

"The Merchant of Venice," she said. "Shakespeare. Ain't that right, Evan?"

I nodded slightly.

"Fuck a bunch of goddamn Shakespeare," Deuteronomy said.

"Well fuck you, then," Chaqueena said. "It's just money. It ain't nothing but a bunch of imaginary ass money, like you need some more."

"Bitch..."

"Don't you bitch me, motherfucker."

Deuteronomy kicked a chest of drawers in his anger. The chest shattered against the wall.

"These motherfuckers ain't got no idea," he said. "Chaque-ena, this ain't nothing bout no money. That motherfucker come in here with his cracker-ass 'I'm a Wharton MBA' bullshit, 'gonna make you all kinds of money,' like I give a damn about his bullshit."

He walked over to me and stuck his face right in front of mine.

"You stupid fucking old man," he said. "You ain't got no idea. Stupid ass been thinking you running drugs all this god-damn time. Like I'm some kind of drug dealer."

He laughed in my face. His breath smelled of alcohol. And pot smoke.

"What- you think this the goddamn year 2000? You living in the past, fool. We ain't get all this money selling dope. We get it off the Internet. Imaginary money."

He stood with pride.

"You ain't been running dope for me," he said. "You just been running a little side cash for me. A little money we turn into paper for a while before we turn it back into electrons."

Portia looked positively mystified. This conversation had to be blowing her mind.

Hell, I was mystified.

"I'm a goddamn hacker, fool," Deuteronomy said. "I been stealing money on the Internet so goddamn fast I can't figure out what to do with it. This bullshit you've been bringing in, we have thugs take it out of ATM's in Eastern Europe and the Car-ibbean. We transfer some money into some accounts, take the limit off a ATM, and get some local thug to draw the cash out for us. He get a little cut, we get most of it, and we send it in with your stupid ass every year or so. Just a little trick to make it disappear for a while. Make it harder to trace."

"It ain't the biggest part of what we do," he said, "but it ain't bad."

How the hell did he do that? I wondered. I couldn't ask, though. I had a ball taped in my mouth.

"You know how we make sure those thugs bring us all the money they get out the machines?" Deuteronomy asked, leaning down again toward my face.

"Because if they don't," he grinned, "we catch em, and we cut their balls off. And their dicks. And we stuff em up their ass. And we leave them out where the other thugs get the message. Clear as day."

Portia screamed into her rubber ball. It sounded really strange. Like some kind of wild animal in the deep forest.

Her face was bright red. She began sobbing. She was choking on her ball.

Chaqueena said nothing.

"You ain't got a fucking clue, Evan Marshall" Deuteronomy said. "You ain't got the first goddamn clue what it is to be me. This between the world and me. It ain't nothing you can even dream of."

Chaqueena was listening intently.

"You think you can fuck this beautiful lady," Deuteronomy said. "She young enough to be your granddaughter. And guess what, she already in love. She in love with a black man. And all you want to do is go over to her apartment and fuck her. Want to go to the strip club and watch her dance naked, swinging that pretty pussy right up in front of your fat, white face."

No one argued with him.

"She think you her goddamn teacher. She think you the only white motherfucker ever gave a damn about her, stead of watching her dance at that strip club just to see her swing her little dick around."

Portia was... I can't find words to describe her facial expression at this point.

"Here's what the problem is," Deuteronomy said. "Here's what you don't know. It's all over for your white ass, Evan. You see me and Chaqueena here, we the future. We what's coming, what your children and your grandchildren gonna be living with. We all you got coming in the world. And you and your kind been stealing from niggers and killing them and cutting they fucking balls off long as they been white people on the planet Earth."

I could hear myself breathing heavily. I could see panic in Portia's eyes. She was whimpering.

"He's right, Evan," Chaqueena said. "You know he's right. He's not particularly articulate, I'll admit, but he's going straight to the point."

I could, of course, say nothing in response.

"You've thought you were superior to him ever since you knew he existed," Chaqueena said. "You thought you were superior to me, for God's sake. You don't think we felt that? You think we couldn't smell it on you?"

Portia's body was quaking in violent tremors.

"Do you even realize I'm about to graduate from college?" Chaqueena said. "I've been accepted to Duke Law School, Evan. After all these years you've known us, do you really know anything about us?"

"Chaqueena," Deuteronomy said. "You wasting your breath on these two. They ain't never gonna understand."

"Oh," Chaqueena said, "I think Evan is going to understand. I think we're going to get him there."

64

Chaqueena knelt in front of my chair.

Her face was right in front of my crotch. "I mean look at you, Mr. Evan Marshall. You an educator. You care about the black people you run into. You lift them up to a higher plane of existence. You enlighten them.

"Give me the box cutter," she said.

Deuteronomy handed her a red box cutter. She slid her thumb on the button to project the razor blade.

"Evan," she said. "I really thought you loved me."

She looked straight into my eyes.

"And I thought I loved you," she said.

She could get my answer without the words.

"I can see the love," she said. "But I can see that same kind of love when you look at your wife, too."

She turned toward Portia.

"And I can see it when she looks at you," Chaqueena said.

There was silence here. Portia was shivering.

"And you know how much I love Deuteronomy."

I nodded.

"There's all this love, then, but there's all this violence," Chaqueena said.

"And crime," she said.

"And fucking...

"And stealing...

"And hurting...

"That stuff is real, too, ain't it Evan?" she said. She paused for an answer. But I couldn't answer, of course.

"Are we just imagining all that stuff?" Chaqueena said.

She lifted the red box cutter in her fist and propped her fist on my thigh. She looked into my eyes for the answer. But I couldn't give it to her.

I wanted so badly to be able to say something useful here— anything true that would make things better.

"You've always wanted another go with me, haven't you, Evan?" Chaqueena said.

She gently took my scrotum in her hand and pulled it lovingly toward her. I slid across the chair to follow the motion, as much as the duct tape would allow me to move.

"I bet your wife don't know about my little secret, do she?" Chaqueena said.

She turned to Portia.

"Do you know I have a dick?" Chaqueena asked her.

Portia stopped crying.

"Yes," Chaqueena said. "I've got a dick. And I've got a pussy. That's for real. Evan didn't tell you about that?"

"You probably didn't even think that kind of thing was even real," Chaqueena said.

Portia was wildly silent.

"She doesn't know about our video, does she?" Chaqueena said to me.

And now I was erect. My penis was red and glaring and pointed at the heavens.

Deuteronomy spoke up. "What you need, Evan," he said, "is an attitude adjustment."

"What you need," Chaqueena said, "is a greater understanding of the mystery of the universe."

Chaqueena tilted my erection toward the sky and kissed my scrotum.

Portia screamed again into her rubber ball.

"I don't mean to hurt you, Evan," Chaqueena said. "It's going to hurt terribly for a moment, but then you can step out of that mental straitjacket and see the things you've never seen before. You can understand people so much more."

She gently stroked my erection.

"Look at that little hard-on," she said.

She licked the tip of my erection.

I almost ejaculated.

"You can't see outside of the classifications, can you?" Chaqueena said. "Maybe it would help you to step outside the classifications yourself. Maybe you could just be."

She readied the box cutter for the surgery.

I was crying now.

"As Krishna told Arjuna," she said, preparing to cut through the scrotum, "the real enemies are desire and anger. You need to focus on that."

I was shaking uncontrollably.

"You'll find," she said, and she looked up at me with that beatific smile, "that it's... Oh how can I describe it? I can't find the words, Deuteronomy."

She was paused in deep contemplation, with the box cutter poised, ready to cut.

She kissed my balls again.

"Fuck it," Chaqueena said to me with the most beautiful smile. "It's ineffable. It's fucking ineffable."

As she began the surgery, I screamed into the rubber ball.

When she stuck her fingers in to pluck my testicles out, I passed into unconsciousness.

65

In hindsight, it's really not that terrible a procedure.
With a LOT of hindsight.
With about three years' worth of hindsight.
I imagine, with proper anesthetic and antibiotics...
My grandfather was diagnosed with prostate cancer when he was in his late seventies. The recommended course of treatment for an elderly man, in the late Twentieth Century, was castration.

(Primarily for emotional reasons, this is no longer the case. Even though recent medical evidence indicates the treatment is often the most effective and safe remedy, surgical castration has become extremely rare.)

Removing the testicles would slow the growth of the cancer, the doctors told him, so he would in all likelihood die of something else.

In the end, they were correct.

After he had his surgery, he told me something I've always remembered. I was a very young man when he said this to me.

"I've always thought," my grandfather told me, "that God isn't fair at all."

He had a twinkle in his eye. "He just doesn't make sense."

"The way it ought to be," he said, "is when a man gets old, his hair and teeth ought to stay in, and his balls ought to fall off."

Your grandfather says some things you don't really appreciate for a few decades.

Now I'm sitting in my study, writing this. My Labrador is lying on the rug at my feet. He turns onto his back and sticks his legs in the air. He is no more troubled by his alteration than I am. In fact, we are both happier creatures, truth be told. There's so much we just don't have to worry about any more.

Portia seems to like me more these days, too. Why in the world did she stay with me? How could she possibly forgive me for what I put her through?

But forgiveness came. It came out of nowhere. I may even have begun- is it possible to say this?- I may have begun to forgive myself.

For God's sake, if Portia can find a way to forgive me and love me...

But Portias are sort of beyond-

They are sort of just beyond what we would imagine. They are off in that realm of the Shakespearean heroine, off in that mystery...

Portia's sex drive is much diminished with age. What remains of it can be satisfied with those tricks I still have at my disposal. But our relationship isn't about sex. It's about love.

It's the guy Portia lives with that seems to hold her attention more. The guy she forgave for the unforgivable.

It is a mystery, I realize.

I don't have to carry shipments for Deuteronomy Jackson these days, thank God. I just go on sailing trips with Portia and my friends. We just enjoy the sailing.

And I don't daydream about molesting my college students. I actually get to concentrate on Shakespeare now when I'm teaching a class, instead of those short skirts and nineteen-year-old legs in the front row.

Well... I don't daydream as much.

Strangely, very strangely I think, I've gotten involved in the Black Lives Matter movement. I can't quite tell where that comes from. You'd think... For God's sake you'd think...

It's easier to imagine I might vote for Donald Trump for President, right?

Isn't that easier to imagine?

Enough, already!
Why don't you just try to get a grip on reality?

The End

The name that can be named is not the enduring and
unchanging name...
Always without desire we must be found,
if its deep mystery we would sound

- Tao Te Ching

Also by Marshall Evans

The Wheelman: *How the Slave Robert Smalls Stole a Warship and Became King*

Ten Tales of Improbable Escape: *Stolen from the Thief Giovanni Boccaccio*

Available wherever books are sold.

www.MarshallEvans.net